WHEN THE TIME COMES

BY AMONI HAYNES

When The Time Comes
By Amoni Haynes

WHEN THE TIME COMES

CHAPTER 1
WORLD OF TROUBLE

Forrest Gump said that life is like a box of chocolates. You never know what you're gonna get. I couldn't agree more with that statement. Life has so many ups and downs, and every day never turns out to be the same—or do they? Well, for most of my childhood, every day was the same. When I was younger, I saw people on television—mainly celebrities—place such a high value on things such as money and looks, but as a little boy in Westchester County, NY, those things never really crossed my mind. I could just hang out all day every day and enjoy myself, whether it was through playing video games, watching Spongebob, or something else.

I didn't have to worry about money because, legally, I couldn't work, and my parents made sure we always had a roof over our heads and food to eat. I also never paid attention to looks, whether it was somebody's race or how physically appealing they were, because I just wanted to have fun. The only things that crossed my mind daily were the well-being of my family and my overall happiness. My family is my everything. My mom, dad, and two brothers— my fraternal twin, Kevin, and my younger brother, Cameron, AKA Lil Man—are my motivation to get through each day. They bring me happiness, but I started to see things change as I got older and reached middle school.

I attend school in a suburban neighborhood where my family and I are definitely not part of the majority. We for sure stick out like sore thumbs because there aren't many black people in the town. My mom was born in New York, and my dad was born in St. Ann's, Jamaica. He came to this country when he was eighteen. My parents worked extremely hard to allow us to live in this nice area, but because of where we live and how we look, my parents had to talk to Kev and me about possible prejudice and bias we may endure in school.

I remember the conversation starting with my mom saying, "AJ, Kevin, my darlings, the two of you are growing up in front of my eyes, and your father and I felt it was time to let you know about some things to expect going into middle school and beyond, so the two of you aren't surprised when something like this comes up."

"That's right, boys. You need to know that as people grow up, their thoughts and opinions might change, and how they might've viewed you when you were little boys probably will be different now. Adults aren't excused either, and if you feel any adult is being prejudiced or is harassing you, let us know, and your mother and I will deal with it," my father said to us.

Kevin asked, "What does prejudiced mean?"

"It means that others will have some hurtful opinions of who you are and what you do without actually getting to know you," said my father.

"And we don't mean to scare you two, but we love you so much, and our job as your parents is to prepare you for your journey through life," said my mother.

To be honest, I was confused and scared because I didn't understand why someone wouldn't like me because of how I looked; I didn't want to live my life in fear of being judged. But it was only time until something like this would happen to me, and sure enough, it did.

I was in seventh grade when I first encountered racial prejudice. One of the many similarities my father and I share is a common enemy in seasonal allergies. Around the springtime, my allergies were really bad, and my first-period math teacher, Mr. Jefferson, suspected something else of me. Pollen was my surefire enemy, and my eyes would get red but not bloodshot red. It never affected my vision in any way, and my eyes were never irritated.

Now, Mr. Jefferson thought differently of my condition and had assumptions of what I possibly might've partaken in before class.

"Mr. Hendrix, are you alright?" asked Mr. Jefferson.

I responded, "Of course I am, Mr. J. Why wouldn't I be?"

"Well, you don't seem like it; do you need to go to the nurse's office?"

I said, "No, Mr. J. I feel fine. Can I sit in my seat now?"

Mr. Jefferson responded, "Well, I think you should go to the nurse's office, and I'll call her right now."

I went to the nurse's office and she gave me eye drops to reduce the redness in my eyes.

But this wasn't just a one-time thing. Mr. Jefferson would accuse me of smelling a certain way and then would ask to check my bag every time I came into class. It was embarrassing to have him constantly police me every first period while my classmates just observed the situation at hand. I felt hopeless and didn't believe that this harassment would stop and that a grown man would stop making me feel insignificant for being black. For three weeks, no one stood up for me, so I felt I had to reach out to someone.

I would come home all mopey and my parents would ask why I looked so upset all the time, and I'd always tell them that I was tired or I wasn't feeling good. I figured my parents knew something was going on, but they didn't approach me about it. I remembered what they said during their conversation with my brother and me, and I should've told them, but I was scared. I didn't know how my mother and father would've reacted, and to be honest, it probably would've turned into a one-sided screaming match from them towards Mr. J, and that's not what I wanted. I wanted Mr. Jefferson to feel the same pain I felt for those three weeks, and I knew exactly who would bring that pain onto him.

Instead of letting my parents know what was going on, I went and told Principal Ward. I thought that telling Mr. Jefferson's employer first would escalate the situation, which is what I wanted. I was fed up with Mr. Jefferson's shit. I was tired of feeling less than a human being. I was tired of feeling trapped in a cage like an animal. I was tired of being the victim, and it was time to fight back.

I told him that Mr. Jefferson had been harassing me for the past three weeks by constantly checking my bag without permission and accusing me of smelling a certain way and that it brought me extreme distress and discomfort. Instantly, he told me he would have a talk with Mr. J.

That same day, I got off the bus from school and walked to my front door. Unexpectedly, I was met at the door by my parents.

"AJ, what did I tell you? Why couldn't you come to us first?" asked my father.

I figured Principle Ward let my parents know what I told him before I got home. I said to my father, "Dad, I was going to tell you and Mom what was going on, but I felt that if I told Principal Ward first, it would keep Mr. Jefferson on his toes."

"Well, at least you told an adult, and that's what matters," said my mother.

Deep down, I knew I had a petty mentality. I endured the embarrassment and harassment from Mr. Jefferson, so it was only right to counter back. He might not hear it from me, but he was definitely going to hear it from Principal Ward as well as my mother and father. He'd get an earful from the three of them, but at the end of the day, I desired to see his face after he was terminated because it would mean the embarrassment and the stress would finally be over.

The next day, my parents came in to have a mediation meeting with Principal Ward and Mr. Jefferson, and in my head, I thought Mr. J should just turn in his resignation papers right then and there. The meeting was in the conference room in the principal's office, and I was told to sit in the chair right outside. When the meeting started, I was able to see through the glass windows and hear the entire conversation because the room's walls were very thin.

Between my parents, my mother is the more outspoken one. She's a human megaphone. My mother makes sure that her voice and opinions are heard, and she's never afraid to call people out on their shit. NEVER! She was visibly upset at the harassment Mr. Jefferson placed on me, and she wanted answers.

"Mr. Ward, as you are aware, for the past three weeks, Mr. Jefferson has been harassing my son, and I don't appreciate it at all. It's obvious that he doesn't harass any of the other students, and we all know why."

"Mrs. Hendrix, what are you insinuating?" asked Mr. Jefferson.

"First of all, don't cut off my wife when she's speaking, and second, we know you're a piece of shit. Don't act like you don't know. My wife and I dug up some dirt on you, and I think this is something you need to hear, Mr. Ward," my father said.

Mr. Jefferson replied, "I have no idea what they're talking about."

My mother said, "Oh, really? Well, you wouldn't mind if we showed Mr. Ward, would you?"

Mr. Ward looked at Mr. Jefferson and said, "I would like to see this."

My mother showed Principal Ward a student-teacher harassment story that was published by a local paper in a different school district three years ago about Mr. Jefferson and another student. The article was titled, "High School Math Teacher Files False Police Report on Black Student Over Lost Cell Phone." The article described how Mr. Jefferson falsely accused a black student of stealing his iPhone when it turned out he had left it in his car. The student won a settlement with the school over the situation, and supposedly, Mr. Jefferson resigned before the school's administration could fire his ass. Mr. Ward probably didn't know about this because Mr. Jefferson was referred to as Mr. Lingard at the time, which was his ex-wife's last name (he took his wife's last name at marriage).

Principal Ward was shocked that he and other administration members hadn't known about the situation prior to hiring Mr. Jefferson. He instantly looked at Mr. Jefferson and I could see the fear in Mr. J's eyes. He was completely speechless. At that point in time, he had to be shitting himself as he realized what was to come.

My father then began to speak. "It seems to us, Mr. Ward, that this school has employed an individual who clearly has a racial bias towards black individuals. Now, I'm not sure where this stems from, but if I had to guess, didn't your ex-wife of ten years leave you for a black man, Mr. Jefferson?"

My parents were in a crazy detective mode when it came to Mr. Jefferson, and I loved it! Apparently, the night before, my mom and dad were able to find pictures of his former wife on social media with a new man a couple of months before the police report incident.

Fear turned to anger as Mr. Jefferson got up from his seat and said, "Don't you talk about my wife."

"You mean ex-wife," replied my father.

"Now, Mr. Ward, my husband and I suggest that you fire this man, or we will bring this to the local press, which would not only make you and Mr. Jefferson look horrible but the school in general. I'm sure you don't want this school to have a reputation of being racially biased in this day and age," said my mother.

"That certainly won't be the case, Mr. and Mrs. Hendrix, as Mr. Jefferson won't be working at this school from here on out," said Principal Ward.

Principal Ward escorted Mr. Jefferson out of the conference room as he stormed out of the office and out of the building with a look of frustration. Revenge was absolutely sweet! I knew that it would be hard for Mr. Jefferson to ever get a teaching job again, and to be honest, it brought a little smile to my face. My parents and Principal Ward then exited the conference room and my mother and father took me home.

From my experience with Mr. Jefferson, I now knew that his bias towards me and how he viewed black people came from his former partner leaving him for a black man. What I didn't get was why me? Why the other student he had harassed? Why couldn't he take out his frustration on his wife and her new partner? Mr. Jefferson's bias came from pure jealousy of another individual, and he decided to turn his own insecurities onto others. It was hard to come home every day and feel lesser than my classmates and lesser of a person due to his actions towards me. I knew as a child that his actions were wrong, so why didn't he realize it himself?

Well, I didn't stop dealing with the bullshit as my classmates became the perpetrators. A year later, in my final year of middle school, I participated in career day in my career preparedness class. It was a very interesting class because it had all of us kids think about our futures at an early age. On career day, our teacher, Ms. Peterson, had a couple of individuals with different occupations come in and share presentations about their jobs. An astronaut, a marine biologist, a lawyer, and a Wall Street day trader spoke with our class. The presentations were amazing, and I felt like I walked away with a future career in mind.

"So, class, I hope you all enjoyed the presentations from the experts. Before we end class today, I want to go around the room and have each of you share what you want to be when you grow up."

Ms. Peterson started with Sam Howard, whose parents were well-known attorneys across America. Any musical artist, athlete, or billionaire who has ever gotten jammed up, best believe Sam's parents have represented them.

"I want to be a businessman when I'm older because I love money," said Sam.

Ms. Peterson then asked Jessica Howard, whose father was DJ Demo, known as the best EDM DJ in the world, and she told Ms. Peterson, "I want to be an actress and a model when I grow up."

I could see why she'd want to be an actress and model. She was very attractive, and all the guys in our grade wanted to talk to her. Plus, her dad had so many industry connections that could make her dreams come true at any time.

Ms. Peterson went around the class to other students and finally got to me. "Well, AJ, what do you want to be when you grow up?"

"Well, Ms. P., I think I want to be an astronaut!" I said.

I told her how cool it would be to go into a spaceship and land on the moon and explore all of the wonders of the galaxy. The astronaut's presentation had me tied up and ready to go to space, but someone had something to say about my newfound aspirations.

"AJ, as an astronaut, I don't think so. Why don't you think about being a rapper or a basketball player? I'd bet you'd be good at that. My parents represent a lot of those people, and they look just like you, AJ!" said Sam.

I looked at Sam from across the classroom with anger because I felt how dare he tell me what I should be. I wanted to be an astronaut! I didn't want to rap or play ball; I wanted to take off to space.

"Now, Sam, you can't decide what AJ wants to be; only AJ can decide," said Ms. Peterson.

I kept saying in my mind, "I want to be an astronaut, I want to be an astronaut." All of a sudden, I screamed out loud, "I want to be an astronaut! Sam, why do I have to rap or hoop, huh? Why can't I put on a jumpsuit and take off to space? What makes you feel like you can tell me what the fuck I want to be, Sam?"

My outburst was met with pure silence. I looked across the room and everyone, even Sam, looked shocked. Everybody knew me as the quiet and reserved kid in the class, so my eruption caught them off guard and showed them a different side of me that they never knew. I knew it was very uncharacteristic of me to go all out like that, but for some reason I was just built up with pure anger and frustration with Sam.

Immediately, Ms. Peterson told me to leave the room. "AJ! That kind of tone and language will not be tolerated in this classroom, and I'll have to ask you to leave as a teacher's aide escorts you to Principal Ward's office," she said.

I exited the classroom and was escorted by one of the TAs to the office. As we were walking, I actually felt good about what I did and almost forgot about it. At that point in time, I just wanted to go home and see my family. I knew I would hear about it from my parents, but I knew a punishment of a week, a month, or however long they would punish me for wouldn't diminish the love that they had for me.

We got to Principal Ward's office, and he was sitting there waiting for me.

"Mr. Hendrix, come take a seat."

I sat down, and Principal Ward discussed what my punishment would be. While he was talking, my arm felt a little tingly, and then it started to reflect this crazy blue luminescence throughout it, and I instantly jumped out of the chair and shrieked.

Principal Ward then said, "Mr. Hendrix, what is the problem?"

At that moment, I realized two things: One, I was for sure possessed with something, and two, Principal Ward definitely thought I was crazy.

I said, "I'm okay, Principal Ward."

"Okay, good. As I was saying, you'll receive two weeks of lunch detention for the foul language used in Ms. Peterson's class, and you'll write a letter of apology to her as well for disrupting her class. I will also, as you probably know, let your parents know of your actions today," he said.

I went home later that day, and my parents laid down my punishment. They took my video games away for a month, and I couldn't watch *Friday Night Smackdown* with Kevin for a month. Those were two things that I really enjoyed partaking in. They took away the stress and the worry I had with reality because I could just focus on having fun. For that entire month, I struggled with not being able to enjoy those things, but it also gave me time to wonder what that thing was shining out of my arm.

CHAPTER 2
NEW ADJUSTMENT

My middle school years were over, and it was time for high school. I hadn't seen that blue light in my arm since the first time, and my anxiety, fear, frustration and all of the emotions I felt prior were gonna get worse. Yeah, I was mad back then that I was being judged because of the color of my skin, and it really killed my self-esteem, but I took that time to realize that my skin tone was something I couldn't change. What I was fearful of and not prepared for was the possibility of getting bullied physically and verbally. I was really small and frail coming into the ninth grade, and I knew that I'd be an easy target to be picked on, especially by some seniors. My brother didn't have to worry about being bullied because he had both the brains and the muscle; nobody—regardless of what they looked like—was going to pick on him. I had the brains but not the muscle, and my brother couldn't be there with me every step of the way, so I was kinda screwed.

Besides resembling a human stick figure, I definitely wasn't the most appealing to the eye. Physically, I resembled Steve Urkel without the glasses and with braces. I was in high school now, so my interests changed from playing video games and watching cartoons to lusting over women! There were so many beautiful girls in our school that I couldn't count them all on my fingers, but I knew they wouldn't look my way, so why bother, right?

The first couple of weeks were hard. My books got slapped out of my hands by jocks multiple times, I got robbed of the lunch money my parents gave me each week, and I got rejected by a girl I had a crush on. At the end of each day, I went home, ran straight to the bathroom and took a good look at myself in the mirror, with the self-doubt hitting me instantly like a Deontay Wilder knockout punch.

To be honest, all I wanted to be was a popular kid. I wanted to be a jock with veins popping out of my biceps. I would've loved to have a multitude of people yearning to be my friend. I would've loved not to have a fear of being picked on or bullied, and of course I wanted all the girls on my body, but the mini-me inside my mind would say, "AJ, you're not good enough."

My desires for my high school experience didn't come to fruition, and my worst nightmare unfolded. In high school, kids from grades 9-12 shared a gym class, and yes, gym was mandatory. We also had to share locker rooms, meaning little ninth graders like me were in the same locker room as the jocks, and it was hell. We had to change every day, and that was where I was most vulnerable. The jocks would whip people, especially the younger kids, with their shirts and would try to embarrass us by pantsing us while we were in our boxers.

Sadly for me, I was in the same class as the football players and the quarterback, Jetson Hardy. He was a tall, stocky dude with an ego out of this world, and he was an asshole. One day, we had just finished gym and went down to the locker room to change. Following me down the steps were Jetson and his football buddies. They closed the locker room door and got right to work. They took off their t-shirts and started whipping kids left and right as hard as they could and pantsed the kids who were in the midst of changing. I was scared, so I ran to the other side of the locker room, hoping they would stop, but I heard the noise of the whiplash get louder and louder. I had to change quickly because, for one, the bell was going to ring in five minutes, and two, I didn't want to get pantsed.

I rushed to take my gym shirt and shorts off, but before I could do that, I heard someone shout, "Hey, nerd," in my direction. It was Jetson and his dumbass football crew. Jetson said to me, "Where do you think you're going?"

With him and the crew towering over me, I said, "Guys, I really don't want any trouble. May I just change in peace?"

Jetson and his boys started laughing. I was in a vulnerable state, barefoot in my boxers with my skinny legs.

They got closer, and I was in fight-or-flight mode. My heart was beating super loud and fast. My head was a bouncing basketball, and I was panting like a mad man. I wondered why Jetson found pantsing a male and seeing their bare ass amusing.

He looked at me and asked, "What did you say to me?"

At that moment, I realized I had said what I thought out loud without knowing. Out of pure adrenaline, I responded, "Man, fuck that. Do what you gotta do, pussy. I can't be late to class."

The sheer evil look in his eyes was truly scary as they lit up in a devilish fashion. His body started twitching and flailing, and a demonic spirit possessed his body. Jetson had sharp, jagged teeth and bloodshot red eyes, and he started to yell at me in a deep voice. "You know what? I should snap your dirty, skinny, black ass in half like a twig. Do you know who you're talking to?"

I thought, *Here we go again. I'm seeing shit!* First, the blue light coming from my arm, and now this. I was in utter disbelief at what I saw. I was so scared that I pissed my boxers right in front of them. My eyes were wide open, and I had no real facial expression. I blurted out, "You're a demon! You're a demon! Stay away from me, you devil!"

Everyone in the locker room heard the commotion and scurried over to the other side of the locker room. All I saw were phones and camera flashes as they focused on me.

Jetson was fuming and exhaling heavily; his teammates saw both of us in extreme distress and pulled him back. My arms and legs were wobbling and felt like noodles.

All of a sudden, Blake James, our star running back and Jetson's buddy, stepped in and yelled to everyone, "Hey everybody, just get back to what you were doing. There's nothing to see here."

Everyone who was recording left and went up the stairs to the main floor. Blake looked at Jetson and said, "Yo, Jetson, get your fucking act together. It's not even worth it."

Jetson looked at him, and then he and the rest of the jocks went up the stairs as well while Blake stayed back with me.

He told me, "Don't mind him. He's just mad that his girl broke up with him last night."

Still in shock, I managed to utter some words out while stuttering, "T-t-t-thanks, man. You d-d-didn't have to do that."

He responded, "It's alright, AJ. You're not the only one tired of his bullshit."

The bell was about to ring, which meant a transition to my next class was about to happen.

Blake asked, "You want me to walk you to your class, AJ? You know, because Jetson might try to sneak you."

I responded, "Yeah, that's fine. Do you know where English 105 is?"

He said he did, and we proceeded to the classroom. It felt really good to know that there were still decent people existing in the school. I felt vulnerable because I didn't have my brother there to back me up, and Blake saw that and stood up for me.

We went up the steps, and Jetson wasn't there, so we continued towards English 105. While we were walking, I felt a little off from what happened, and Blake could see that.

"You sure you're okay, bro?" he asked.

I sighed in distress. "To be honest with you, no, not at all. I've been having a hard time fitting in, I can't seem to relax, and on top of that, I've been seeing weird shit lately. Agh! I don't know what's wrong with me, man."

"Welcome to high school, man. It can be stressful at times," he said.

English 105 was right around the corner, and Blake was gearing to say his goodbye for the day. Before we got to the classroom door, three beautiful girls walked by and one of them said hi to Blake.

Blake looked at her and said, "Katie, don't talk to me, please!"

I was absolutely shocked! A girl like that would never give me the time of day, but Blake just turned her down like it was nothing.

I looked at him and asked, "Dude, what was that?"

He looked at me and said, "AJ, that's Jetson's ex-girl. She's trifling, trust me. You don't want to talk to her. She might look good, but looks are deceiving, my friend."

I asked how so and he told me, "The reason she and Jetson broke up was because she was texting me while they were 'going through tough times.' I had to tell him because that's wrong—you feel me?—and she broke up with him knowing I was gonna tell him, regardless."

I'd obviously never experienced something like that, but hearing Blake tell me made me feel something like sympathy towards Jetson. We reached the door, and before I said goodbye to Blake, he handed me a small, circular pill.

"Here, take this. It'll not only help you relax, but you'll feel like a whole new person," he said.

"What is this?" I asked.

"It's called 'candy.' It's not really candy, but it tastes like it."

"And you're sure it'll help me out?"

"Yeah, bro. Trust me; you'll feel like a weight was lifted off your shoulders."

I believed what he was saying. Before I entered the classroom, I took the candy—I normally don't take things from strangers because that's what my parents told me, but for some reason, I trusted him.

We dapped each other up, and he said, "I'll see you tomorrow, AJ," as he walked down the hallway and I entered my English class.

I was glad that Blake took the time to stand up for me and get to know me a little; I felt like I had not only a protector but also a true friend, and I was also glad he gave me the candy because he was right! I sat in English class feeling mellowed out, calm, and a little giddy. My teacher kept asking me what was so funny because I couldn't stop giggling, but she eventually ignored me. The best part about it was that I totally forgot about both what happened in the locker room and all of the insecurities I had felt for the past few weeks. I truly felt nothing but happiness!

For the majority of the year, Blake and I were really close friends. Not only was he supplying me with candy, but he was taking the time to get to know me. My freshman year had started off rocky, but it ended pretty well.

Blake was a senior the following year, and he let me sit with the older kids at his lunch table every day. He introduced me as his friend and hyped me up to make me seem like a cool person, and honestly, it felt amazing! I got attention from girls who never used to look my way, people knew who I was, and he even gave me the nickname Slender Bender. It felt great, but Blake was headed to play football across the country at USC at the end of the year.

I was gonna miss having that one friend in school. My brother and I didn't have any classes or lunch periods together, so I was gonna be all alone again once Blake left. I also didn't know how I was going to get more of the candy if Blake wasn't going to be in New York. I didn't want to go back to being the depressed, insecure and mentally unstable human being I was before I took it. The candy allowed me to be free! I was able to eliminate all distractions and just live, so I had to ask him where he got it from.

A week before the end of sophomore year, I was at lunch with Blake and his friends, and everyone was signing each other's yearbooks. As Blake was signing them, I tapped him on the shoulder.

"Hey, Blake, is it alright if I talk to you for a minute?"

"Yeah, sure, AJ. What's up?"

We walked a distance away from people so no one could hear what we were talking about.

"Blake, I just want to say thank you for everything that you've done for me. You really helped me build my confidence up and helped me out of a tough time."

"Don't mention it, AJ! I was once you like you, man, so I know when someone is in need of a friend. Plus, I know you like the candy. It seems like it's working for you."

"Yeah, I wanted to ask you about that as well. I know we probably won't be seeing each other for a while, and I wanted to know where you get that stuff from?"

"I can't really tell you where or who I get it from, but I actually have to get rid of my last supply cuz' I can't take this shit with me to college."

He went into his bag and pulled out a huge Ziploc bag filled with candy. My eyes lit up like a tree on Christmas!

Blake continued, "So, AJ, I'll tell you what. Normally, I charge people 200 bucks for this much, but I need to get rid of it fast, and I know you really like this shit, so I'll give it to you for 100 bucks. It should last you about a year, so don't take more than you should."

I was listening to Blake but not listening, if you know what I mean, and that was the worst decision I ever made in my life. Just looking at the bag, I instantly remembered how good the candy made me feel and how it tasted; I could only imagine what taking two or three a day would make me feel like. A hundred dollars did seem like a lot, and I was reluctant to cough up the money, but the voice in my head told me to do it, so I did. I ended up giving Blake half of the money I made shoveling decks around the neighborhood during the winter, and he gave me the bag of candy.

That summer, I blew through the bag that Blake gave me. When I woke up each day, I took two or three from the dresser, where I hid them so I wouldn't let my parents know I had them. I felt like I was on cloud nine all throughout the day but would completely crash at night. I was so out of it that I couldn't even have dinner at the table with my family. My parents and brothers would ask me what was wrong, and I would just tell them that I was sick or not in the mood to eat because I didn't want to believe the candy was doing this to me.

Things started to get worse as I began to develop stomach cramps and immense vomiting, and I couldn't sleep at night. My family was truly scared that I was slowly dying, and I was. A few hospital trips later, the doctors managed to find out what was wrong, and I was extremely nervous because I knew they were going to tell my parents I was taking the candy.

To keep a long story short, the doctor found high levels of canditrophil, also known as "candy," in my system. My parents were in complete distress, filled with anger, frustration and disappointment. They couldn't understand why I would do such a thing and how I got the candy, but I couldn't fork up the energy to tell them.

Because of my addiction, doctors suggested my parents put me in rehabilitation for the whole summer. While I was in rehab, I dealt with horrible withdrawals, my parents and brothers didn't talk to me as much, and my life was in such a downward spiral at 15 years old that I thought it was pretty much over. I felt like a failure—like I let my family down and let my insecurities get the best of me. I tried to use the candy as a way to bury myself and hide from my insecurities, but it only made things worse.

Fast forward a few months to the present, October 23, 2025, and I'm a 16-year-old recovering addict in my junior year of high school. My grades are piss poor, and I have no motivation for school whatsoever. The only thing going for me right now is that I've repaired my relationship with my family, and they've started to regain trust in me.

One day, math class had just ended and lunch was next. I was really hungry and anxious to get out of my least favorite class. As I left, I ran down the second-floor staircase and darted towards the cafeteria. Once I got there, I sat at the table farthest from anybody else and pulled out the turkey sandwich I had made for lunch. Being in rehab for a while didn't give me the opportunity to connect with other people and build friendships, and trying to make conversations gave me bad anxiety, so I was back by my lonesome once again.

The one thing that felt a little off was the noise level in the cafeteria, and to be honest, it had been off for a while. Every year that I'd been in high school, I had lunch with Jetson Hardy, and he was always the loudest person in the lunchroom. I mean, if you were all the way in Australia, you could hear Jetson—that's how loud he was. But it had been fairly quiet every lunch period for the past month, and I wondered what had happened to him. Maybe he switched lunch periods; I don't know.

As time passed, some kids decided to turn on the television in the room, and I don't know why they did because the only channel available was the boring-ass channel 2 global news. Granted, nobody really watched the news unless they showed something shocking or really important, and surprisingly today was that day. A reporter was covering a breaking news story with a title at the bottom that said, "Star NY high school quarterback isolated in state psych ward due to newfound virus."

It had everyone questioning who the fuck it could be.

That question was soon answered as the reporter went on to speak. "I'm here today at NY state's top psychiatric facility, where 50 of the nation's top doctors are analyzing a new virus found in Jetson Hardy, a NY teenage football star. They have characterized the disease as a 'killer virus.' "

The camera switched from the reporter to footage inside of the psych ward, and there was Jetson. Everyone was in complete shock and scared of what they were seeing. Jetson was swinging back and forth, screaming and banging on the plexiglass in his isolation pod, while the doctors stood around observing. I looked closely at the TV and saw the red eyes in Jetson that I had seen when the demon popped out of him, but I don't think anybody else saw them.

The reporter continued, "Hardy's family stated that Jetson was 'just like any teenage boy' outside of football, but over time they saw changes in his behavior. His mother said she observed tendencies of antisocial personality disorder such as spending long hours isolated in his room, constant acts of disrespect, extreme hostility, and being truant in regards to school."

The screen then switched over to another reporter interviewing the distressed Mrs. Hardy as she gave an account of how Jetson's behavior changed over time.

"When Jetson started spending a ton of time isolated in his room, we knew something was up. That wasn't normally him. He loved spending time with us around the house, and when we tried to confront him to see what was wrong, he started to get really aggressive. My son's behavior only escalated from there, and he got really violent and physical towards us," Mrs. Hardy said.

She continued, "He would attack my husband when he wouldn't get his way with the kitchen knives and even lunge at me at times. Other times he would attack us just because. Thankfully, my husband is bigger than Jetson, so he's able to restrain him, but it's very scary because it's like a switch. We can't tell when he's his normal self or when he's manipulating us. We took him out of school one day to get him evaluated, but nobody could tell us what was wrong. That same night, I woke up with my husband holding my son in a headlock while Jetson had a knife in his hand. He was trying to stab me in my sleep. We called the authorities afterward, and they locked him in the psych ward that he's in now."

The screen switched back to the first reporter. "Mrs. Hardy said that the family is in complete distress and are scared that they won't ever get the Jetson that they once knew to be again.

"Doctors ran tests on other Hardy family members to see if any of them had the virus as well, but no traces were found, making them even more confused about the virus' origin. Through many tests and surveillance, the medical experts have determined this virus' ability to control the cognitive abilities of the individual and force them to have murderous characteristics and behaviors. I interviewed Dr. Wildes, the head of the World Disease Control Commission and one of the 50 doctors overseeing this rare situation."

The camera transitioned one final time to a one-on-one interview with Dr. Wildes and the reporter.

The reporter went on to ask, "Dr. Wildes, what should the people in the country—or even around the world—know about this new virus?"

Dr. Wildes responded, "Well, the people of America, and everyone else around the world, should be very worried at this point. This virus has extremely dangerous capabilities, and there's a possibility that a small number of other individuals in different parts of the world may be infected without knowing it. While examining Jetson, we saw that his main intention was to kill all the doctors in the room, but in the slickest way. His IQ numbers are off the charts, which allows him to be very manipulative. He also has top-tier skills that eclipse even the world's best professional mercenaries. Overall, this virus is creating extremely dangerous and inhuman-like killers. As you already know, we were unable to determine the origin of the virus, whether it was manmade by a wretch of a human being or not, but it is here to destroy the human race as a whole. Speaking to all global leaders, for the safety and the best interest of the people, I am announcing a worldwide lockdown for at least a year's time!"

Everyone in the lunchroom was freaking out! People were screaming and crying, and it was complete chaos. The district administration got a hold of our principal fast, and within ten minutes, everyone was either taking off in their whips or hopping on the buses to go home.

I sat in the front seat of the bus with my brother, and with this whole situation unraveling, he looked at me and said, "AJ, I'm really scared of what's going to happen. Are you scared?"

I responded, "Yeah, Kevin, I'm really scared. I'm worried about you and me, I'm worried about Mom and Dad and Lil Bro, and I'm worried about this whole thing in general. I don't want any of us catching this virus and trying to kill each other, you feel me? But, all we can do is pray and hope for the best."

We rode the bus for another ten minutes until it got to our stop. Our parents and younger brother greeted us with a huge hug, grabbed our hands and brought us into the house as fast as possible. This worldwide lockdown had come of nowhere and was a complete shock to everyone, and I definitely saw it in my parents. My mom looked at us and patted us down, asking us if we were okay or if we felt weird. My brother and I both said we were okay and my mom sighed in relief.

My dad said to us, "Boys, go to your rooms and change so we can wash those clothes."

We went to our rooms and changed. We came back down the steps and our parents and lil bro, Cam, were at the dining room table holding hands. My mom said to us, "You two come join us to pray."

We sat down and joined hands.

My mom began to pray. "Dear Lord, I pray to you on behalf of my family—with this virus and worldwide lockdown among us—that you're able to watch over us and protect our overall physical and mental health. We pray that we can soon return to everyday normalcy and continue to enjoy life the way we are supposed to. We thank you, worship you and are truly blessed and grateful for everything you've done for us. In Jesus' name, I pray—"

We then all collectively said, "Amen!"

After the prayer, we all hugged each other with love and passion as my father reassured us, saying, "Everything is gonna be alright."

Eventually, days turned into weeks and weeks turned into months. It reached a new year—January 1, 2026—and we were still in lockdown. My parents got to spend more time at home —just like a lot of adults—and for people who were unemployed or lost their jobs, the U.S. government provided them with financial assistance. Shelters were required by the government to help the homeless and give them a place to stay, and honestly, hearing that report from the news shocked me.

The government's goal was to truly eliminate the spread of this virus, and I was grateful and surprised that finally, for once, the U.S. government cared for the wellbeing of every individual. Besides that, though, everyday life was a huge adjustment. Everyday activities were at a complete standstill. People couldn't even go to the grocery stores anymore as groceries—even produce—were purchased online from food factories and farms and delivered to your house. I had to give the delivery drivers props that they were risking their lives to make the lives of others better, but in my opinion, I didn't think it was worth it.

If I had to eat processed junk for the year, I would do it just to make their lives a little easier; plus, that would probably kill me faster than the canditrophil almost did.

When it came to school, my bedroom was my classroom, class occurred virtually through computer screens, I had lunch in my dining room, and I honestly just felt trapped.

It wasn't good for my mental state at all, and I started to fall back down the same dark path as when I was recovering in rehab. The feelings of loneliness, fear, anxiety and loss of happiness all came creeping back and my mind started craving the candy again. I began to feel itchy, my mouth got watery and I missed the taste of the candy. I think I was beginning to go through withdrawal again, so I had to find something to distract myself.

I found my television remote and turned on the TV. The first channel to pop up was the news channel, and the first thing I saw was the casualties being reported. I started to panic and ran downstairs to my family.

"AJ, what's wrong, son?" asked my father.

"Yeah, my G, what's going on? You coming down here all bugged out," said Kevin.

"Well, I just turned on the news and they confirmed casualties! I'm freaking scared!" I screamed.

"AJ, calm down, honey. You need to relax, seriously," said my mother.

My family was so calm and under control. I didn't understand how, so I had to ask.

"Mom, I see how you and Dad and Kev and Cam just seem to be all calm and everything, but don't you see and hear what's going on?" I asked.

She replied, "AJ, we all know what's going on, and we do worry about what's going to happen, but we can't dwell on the past or the future. We can only live in the now. Yes, the world is a madhouse, but life is not guaranteed, so we have to make the best of what we got. See, your problem is that you always think of the negatives and live your life in fear, and that's only going to slowly drain you physically and mentally. Just loosen up a bit, and enjoy the time you have now with your family."

She was right, as mothers always are. I was so stuck in thinking about the bad things like not being accepted, being judged, bullied, getting sick, or even dying that I was giving up precious time enjoying life with the people who love me for me. I realized that I needed to make the best of what I had and go on from there.

My mother finished her food, and my brothers and dad had a Snakes and Ladders board game set up, so I decided to join them and play. We played for hours and hours until it was finally time for everyone to go to bed.

Bedtime is my favorite part of any day. It is truly my escape from reality and is a great distraction from myself and all the negativity.

My dreams always consisted of the perfect world. I'd be able to be someone new for hours each night. One night, I could be an astronaut on his way to the moon or a rockstar selling out a worldwide tour, and the next night I could be the greatest athlete on the planet. I could be the most attractive man in the world like Michael B. Jordan, or I could have billions of dollars stacked to the ceiling like Jeff Bezos. My dreams allowed me to enjoy a life in a world where I had no doubts about myself, where everything horrible or despicable was just flushed away. I always knew that in my dreams I would be very well-liked and my confidence would never be six feet under. I knew that I wouldn't have to hear every five minutes that people were dying or suffering. These were feelings that I longed for in real life, but I could never achieve them. If we could all be the person or have the perfect world we dreamt about, life would be so easy and peaceful.

CHAPTER 3
ESCAPE FROM REALITY

That night, I had trouble sleeping. My mind was disassembled like scrambled eggs. I tossed and turned constantly, trying to close my eyes but just couldn't do it. To ease the struggle, I put in my headphones and listened to some music. I closed my eyes and went to sleep.

Minutes later, I was on a beautiful tropical island, leaning back in my beach chair on a bright red sandy beach with my three-story glass house in the background. I had an ice-cold cup of lemonade in my hand while two beautiful women massaged my feet. I stared at the glowing blue ocean without a worry in the world. I went into my house up the spiral steps and went straight to my enormous bedroom. The room had a huge theater-sized flat-screen TV in the front, the rug was furry and white as snow, and the lights changed colors anytime I clapped my hands together. The bathroom was a few steps away from my bed and consisted of gold marble floors and countertops, as well as solid gold sinks, a solid gold tub, and a solid gold toilet. At that moment, I realized this was where I wanted to be. I thought, *AJ doesn't want to leave, ever.*

With my mind on watching TV, I grabbed a white robe and jumped onto the bed. I started sinking into the mattress like I was slowly disappearing in quicksand. I closed my eyes with a huge smile on my face, and all of a sudden, I heard a loud BANG!

In Undertaker-like fashion, I sat up super fast as I resurrected from the dead. I wasn't in the red sandy tropical paradise anymore. I was in Westchester County, in my small room, on my full-sized bed, upset. While I was still in a somewhat sleepy state, I looked towards my left, and the inside of my closet was lit up with colorful luminescent lights. I hoped that I wasn't having a withdrawal episode again, but I was curious at the same time, so I got out of the bed to open the closet doors. I opened them and was met with a rainbow-like circular portal staring me down. I couldn't believe that nobody else in the house heard the loud noise, but I also couldn't believe my eyes! I thought, *AJ, you're still dreaming. It's not real. It's not real, AJ. You're gonna wake up soon.* I rubbed my eyes a couple more times and the portal was still there.

At this point, I had two options. The first was to wake up either my brothers or parents and let them see the portal themselves. At the same time, I was worried the portal would disappear by the time I got any of them to come to the room, so I went with option two. I figured if I went through the portal, I could really determine if I was just crazy or if this futuristic-like object in my closet was real. So, without hesitating any longer, I walked through the portal.

Once I entered, I became a human fidget spinner. The nonstop spinning motion was extremely bothersome; I screamed at the top of my lungs and closed my eyes, still hoping I was in my strange hallucination. The loud spacey sounds surrounding my ears increased my fear and anxiety to the max, and in that exact moment, I didn't know if those few seconds would be the last seconds of my life.

While spinning in the portal, I started to pick up speed on a decline like garbage down a trash chute. I hit the ground fast and opened my eyes. It was pitch black, and I couldn't see anything. Then, suddenly, I was blinded by a spotlight placed on me.

"Hello, AJ." A deep-toned amplified voice said my name all of a sudden, and I became worried. It was like a mysterious god was talking down to me.

I looked everywhere to see if I could spot anybody and then asked, "Who are you? Who are you? Tell me now!"

"My name is Lucious, and I will be your guardian on your path through a new world. Any questions you have, I will answer them for you, as well as offer my advice to you."

"Lucious, what am I doing here? Where am I, Lucious?" I asked.

"Well, let me tell you where you are. You are on the best planet in the entire galaxy!"

"Okay, but you still haven't told me what I'm doing here. I'm scared and I wanna go home now!" I said.

"AJ, we are facing a major crisis, not just within Planet Elise, but within the entire galaxy. You're aware of what's happening on Earth, correct?"

I responded, "Yes, Lucious, I am well aware, but what does that have to do with me being here?"

"AJ, it's hard to explain. All I can say is that you'll definitely stand out compared to the other newcomers," said Lucious.

"Newcomers? There are others?" I asked.

"Yes. Every newcomer enters Elise with a mentor like myself and an introductory event hosted by Madam Serenity, the queen of Planet Elise. That reminds me, you will be able to return home, but for right now, I need you to put on the glasses and earpiece that are not too far in front of you."

All of a sudden, the spotlight drifted away from me and hovered over the earpiece and glasses. I walked over, picked them up and put them on. When I put on the glasses, I saw multiple buttons in front of me through the lenses; I felt a part of some video game.

Lucious' voice suddenly became more clear and closer to my ear. It felt like he was in my head almost, but he was just with me through the earpiece. I then pressed one of the buttons, and Lucious appeared right in front of me. He was about six feet tall with curly hair and piercing brown eyes.

He looked at me and said, "AJ, these glasses are very important, and you must keep them on at all times. They are a necessity for your normal functions within Planet Elise. If you happen to take the glasses off, please don't lose them! They are also your way out of here, so please keep them in a safe place! On the bottom left, you will see an exit button that allows you to return back to Earth. You have eight hours each day to experience the wonders of this beautiful planet. Once the eight hours are up, the exit button will light up to alert you of your immediate exit. You can also choose to reside in this world for the rest of eternity, but to warn you, that decision comes with a price you'll find out eventually. Anyway, we're gonna have to take a ride to the arena in secrecy."

I asked Lucious why we had to be so stealthy and he said, "We just have to be, okay?"

At that moment, a tall steel door appeared in front of me. I opened it, and Lucious and I walked through. I couldn't believe what I saw. There were flying cars, big exotic-looking buildings, colorful lighting, a sky filled with a multitude of colors and a massive number of people walking around. It reminded me of a futuristic Manhattan. The door closed behind us and disappeared, and I cried inside with tears of excitement, joy and confusion. I was so amazed at this new "home" of mine and immediately thought that this was my opportunity to start a new life—a new journey to the happiness that I desired so much.

Suddenly, Lucious snapped his fingers and one of the flying cars in all black randomly appeared with two other cars in front of it. "Get in, AJ. We gotta get going," said Lucious.

I hopped in the car and we took off. When I got in, I saw there was no driver in the front. I asked, "Lucious, how come there's nobody driving this car?"

He told me that all of the vehicles are programmed to take their passengers to their predetermined destination of choice. Looking through the windows of the flying cars, Planet Elise was beautiful. The bright lights and gorgeous people were astonishing.

"Lucious, this place is amazing! The cars fly here, and it's so bright and colorful. I absolutely love it!"

He responded, "I'm glad you like it, AJ, because this is just the beginning. There are many more things to show you about this world."

I still couldn't fathom this new environment I was in. I felt so euphoric over how Elise looked way different and way better than Earth. We continued on our journey to the arena for the introductory event. A few stoplights and right turns later, we arrived. The cars stopped a block away and we were ready to get out of the car, but before we got out, Lucious handed me a black hoodie and hat.

"Put these on, AJ. Put on your glasses and make sure nobody sees your face."

I asked, "Why do I have to wear this stuff, and why can't people see my face?"

"Alright, alright, AJ. You won't know why yet, but you are someone of very high importance on this planet, and as your mentor and your protector, I have to handle you differently than anybody else," said Lucious.

I now understood that I was an important figure on this planet in some way and form, and I had to act and carry myself like an A-list celebrity.

I put on my glasses, the hat and the hoodie, and we exited the car. The doors closed behind us and we were on our way. From a block down, I could see the big welcome sign for the event at the arena, and as we were walking towards it, Lucious tugged my arm and said, "Oh no, we're not going through there. Security is waiting for us through the side entrance."

We turned down one street before the main entrance, and two huge dudes in black suits were standing at the door. We got there and the security guards instantly addressed Lucious. "Lucious, nice to see you again, buddy!"

Lucious responded, "James, Jacob, how've you two been?"

"Same old, same old, you know. Well, enough chit-chat boys; get in there!"

We walked through the door and entered the building. I immediately asked, "Are people here really that friendly, Lucious?"

"Yes, AJ. That's the norm around here. Everybody knows everybody, and everybody wants to get to know everybody, so you'll have an easy time fitting in!"

I told Lucious, "Well, that's great because I'm from New York, and trust me, New Yorkers aren't this friendly."

He asked, "AJ, could you tell me where New York is?"

"Lucious, you mean...."

"Ah, I'm just kidding. I know where New York is. I'm from Houston, Texas! AJ, what you'll learn is that a lot of these individuals come from all over the world, and just like you, they're all here for a reason."

Inside of the building was a giant movie-theater atmosphere, with a Madison Square Garden feel. There was a huge screen all the way in the front, as well as thousands of seats filled with people, and I didn't know where to sit. I looked up and found enlarged holographic representations of myself and Lucious next to each other in the front row with arrows pointing to seats right below them.

"You can take the glasses and hat off if you want, AJ. Everyone here is new to Elise, just like you, so they won't know who you are," said Lucious.

I took them off and we headed towards our seats, but before we got there, we were met by a tall, slender, robot gentleman.

"Hello, newcomer! Welcome to Elise! My name is Jax, and I will be your server for the intro. Anything you want or need such as snacks, food, drinks, tissues, anything, just use this thing right here, and I'll be at your service!"

Jax handed me a remote-like contraption with literally one button labeled "Jax." I guess this introductory meeting was more like a movie screening.

I went on to sit down in my seat. I hit the button to call Jax for some water because I was parched. He was there in less than two seconds with a bottle of water in his hand for me to drink. He then scurried off to assist other people.

I was super excited for the screening because I wanted to learn more about this new world, and maybe, just maybe, I could figure out why I was chosen to be here before Lucious told me.

Lucious said, "In a few moments, you will meet the woman in charge of this beautiful world. Without her, the existence of Planet Elise would be nothing."

Moments later, the entire place went dark except for the front stage. All of a sudden, fireworks went off, confetti exploded in the air, and the stage was lit up with colored smoke bombs. Walking through the smoke was a tall woman with dark hair and a slim figure who resembled a supermodel, and the screen acted as the backdrop to her entrance.

She began to speak and her voice became amplified.

"Welcome, newcomers, to the beautiful, outstanding, and exotic Planet Elise! I am your leader, your observer, your protector, your savior. I am Madam Serenity, leader of Planet Elise! I was once in the same position as all of you, wondering, 'How did I get here?' But, just know you are all here for a reason. Planet Elise has been around for hundreds of years and was created by my ancestors and many of yours, as well. That's right; you are all here because you all come from Elisian ancestry. My ancestors left their original home of Planet Amity with millions of other Amitans and stumbled upon this beautiful world during their travel. After they left, Amity was destroyed by the Iniquitans.

"The Iniquitans are the biggest threat to the entire universe. They are individuals who live on Planet Iniquitous, another planet within the galaxy. For hundreds of years, many of its leaders have attempted to take over the galaxy with the sole purpose of wanting to be the only living people in the universe. They destroyed Amity, and they have tried to destroy Elise for many years but have failed. The former leader of Iniquitous, Knave, launched an attack on Elise as a step towards universal takeover about two decades ago but was stopped in his tracks by our courageous people and ultimately killed in battle. Iniquitous is now ruled by Insecurity, Knave's daughter. She is seeking to avenge her father's death and accomplish what her father wasn't able to."

Madam Serenity pulled down a huge projector screen to show us what Insecurity looked like and what she was capable of. I was confused about why someone would name their daughter Insecurity. Her appearance caught my attention immediately. She was tall, slender, and had beautiful curly hair similar to Medusa, just without the snakes. Her eyes were bloodshot red, and they were very scary to look at. Insecurity was an evil goddess. Her beauty was intimidating, but what she was capable of was even more terrifying.

Madam Serenity continued to speak. "You all have seen what has occurred on Earth, and that is the work of Insecurity and the devils of Iniquitous. Our security team was able to give us intel through their spy work and discover that she is the culprit behind creating the killer virus, as well as collect a sample of the virus. Our top scientists have examined the sample and tested the virus' efficacy. Surprisingly, it's not that high, meaning the virus will dwindle away most likely in the very near future."

Everybody began to cheer, and I saw smiles across the entire arena.

Madam Serenity went on. "How Insecurity was able to infiltrate the virus into Earth is still unknown, but this is why you all, as well as your mentors, will be part of a formidable task force to help defeat Insecurity and the Iniquitans."

The screen then showed in-depth pictures of Insecurity and her science lab where she was constructing this virus and a video of the virus' activity within the stolen sample. The footage had my stomach in knots. The virus looked like a bunch of black slimy worms squirming around the small vial trying to get out, and it was disgusting to watch.

"Our scientists and security team are going to work extra hard to develop defense technology to protect our fellow Elisans and our friends on Earth and to preserve the universe's existence. As you return to Earth, expect to see things progressing. As mentioned before, a sense of normalcy will be temporarily reinstated on Earth, but it won't be for long as we don't know exactly when Insecurity will strike. Anyway, as this introduction comes to an end, all I have to say is 'It's your time.' Enjoy the wonders of Elise while you're here, but be prepared to fight for the peace and prosperity of the universe like your life depends on it."

Our short introduction to Planet Elise ended, and people began to file out of the arena to explore more of what this new world had to offer.

"AJ, now that you've gotten to know a little bit about this planet, let me show you around a bit," said Lucious.

"Yeah, I would like that," I said.

We walked out through the same door we came through, said goodbye to the security guards, and went on our way.

CHAPTER 4
PERFECT TIMING

Now it was time for me to take a look around Planet Elise with Lucious. We hopped back in the secret service cars from the side door, took a left and headed down a busy street. The cars flew by at super-fast speeds, and people entered and exited them within seconds. A few blocks later, we reached a stoplight, and I turned my attention to four huge bubble fixtures that sat side by side. Inside the capsules were a bunch of little kids utilizing technological hardware and science lab equipment.

Lucious sensed that I was glancing over at the bubbles and said, "Those right there are the evolution stations. As you can tell, our planet is shaped heavily by evolutions in science and technology. So through I.Q. testing, we bring in the most intelligent Elisian-born children to help create new tech and develop new scientific research systems for our planet's development."

"Wow, Lucious. That's amazing! So these kids are learning to be like futuristic doctors and mechanics?" I asked.

He responded, "Exactly, AJ."

Eventually, we continued to drive around Elise, and I saw a building that looked like a futuristic Staples Center and was labeled Elise Recreational Center. It had all-glass walls and a multitude of floors. Lucious saw that I was staring at the rec center and he asked me if I wanted to take a peek inside. I told him yes.

He said, "We can go in, but still keep a low profile. The glasses, hat, and hoodie stay on at all times, got it?"

"I understand, Lucious," I said. Lucious then signaled to the driver to let us out and assured him everything was going to be alright. The driver then pulled to the side, let us out, and we went on our way towards the building.

We reached the front of the rec center and entered through the door on the first floor, which led into the fitness area. There were a bunch of people lifting weights with robots just like Jax wiping and cleaning the equipment. There were also people running these geeked-up treadmills with fancy buttons that measured the runners' heights, weights, and wingspans and predetermined their heart rates and what speed they should be running at. I tasked Lucious where the basketball courts were.

"They're on the tenth floor, which is the top floor, and I'm pretty sure you'll love them when we get there," said Lucious.

He walked with me towards the elevator, and we went on our way to the tenth floor. Besides the first floor, the rec center had a floor for almost every sport imaginable— soccer, baseball, football, track and field, hockey—but of course, I wanted to go to the basketball court because that was my favorite sport. Finally, we reached the tenth floor with the basketball arena on the rooftop. The courts had a nightlife feel with neon lights that lit all four of them up. It was a pretty cool sight to see. We walked out of the elevator and it was jam-packed! Thousands of people surrounded the one court in the middle, and the other three courts were empty.

"Hey, AJ, I know you wanna go over to check out what's going on, but there are a lot of people over there, and I think we should turn back around," said Lucious.

I heard what Lucious said, but I ignored him. It was getting really rowdy and seemed exciting, so I had to check it out!

I took off to the main court and all I heard was him saying, "AJ, get back here," while he chased me. I couldn't see who was on the court at first, so I began to push my way forward. I got to the front to where I could see, and on the court were nine dudes and this goddess to the eye.

My goodness, she was absolutely stunning. She was tall and tan with dark hair, and the fact that she could play basketball made me crush even harder. She was killing the competition out there, sinking shots left and right and breaking peoples' ankles like their shoes were tied together, all while looking like a gift from heaven.

As I stared at the beauty of an angel, someone bumped into me. I went flying like three feet. I rubbed my shoulder as I felt a little pain and got up. My glasses and hat were on the floor, and I picked them up, put my hat on, and shoved my glasses in my pocket. When I rose, I suddenly realized I was on the hardwood. The entire game stopped. I looked up as everyone stared at me, and the ball magically rolled to the bottom of my leg.

Out of embarrassment, I apologized for disrupting the game. The girl and two of her teammates were in front of me, so I continued to apologize.

"Guys, I am so sorry to interrupt your game. I didn't mean to come on the court, really."

All of a sudden, one of the guys in front of me said, "Oh mon Dieu, c'est l'élu!"

Then the other one said, "¡Dios mío, es el elegido!"

I was startled because I obviously didn't understand what they had said and didn't know if it was good or bad, so I froze. I then heard chatter from the thousands of people surrounding the court, and I began to feel very nervous. In my mind and gut, I had a feeling something bad was about to happen.

Finally, the girl began to speak. "Nicolas, Sebastian, shush!" She raised her right hand and made a balled fist, and every single person in the arena except for me got on one knee and bowed their heads. I knew I fucked up at that moment. This girl held some authority to draw a reaction from thousands of people like that, and I figured my short time on Planet Elise was over. With the silence in the crowd surrounding the arena, I heard Lucious' fast-paced footsteps approaching. He was jumping over the kneeled crowd to find out where I was until we locked eyes from a distance.

I mouthed to him, "I'm sorry," and then he ran to the center court where I was stuck in one place like Lady Liberty.

Lucious got on one knee and said, "My apologies, Your Highness. AJ here didn't mean to interrupt your game. We'll just be on our way out." He pulled my arm, and I went down on one knee as well and bowed my head.

"No need, Lucious. It's okay. He doesn't know who he is, does he?" asked the girl.

Lucious replied, "No, he does not, Your Highness. I was going to bring it up to him in due time."

"Well, AJ, my name is Phoenix, and we'll have a chat after the game's over."

I was absolutely confused about what was going on. How did I not know who I was? I was AJ Hendrix, a 16-year-old boy from New York—what else about myself did I not know?

"Let's play ball, guys! Fifteen to fourteen, game point us," said Phoenix.

Everyone got up off their knees and started to cheer again. Lucious pulled me off of the court aggressively and we went to the bathroom. He turned on the lights, locked the door and gave me a death stare.

"AJ, what the hell are you doing? You don't understand how big of an opportunity this is for me. I can't have you messing things up," he said.

"My apologies, Lucious. I just wanted to see what was going on," I said.

My curiosity had almost got Lucious in trouble with Elisian royalty and I felt bad. I promised Lucious that I would listen to him more often and that would never happen again. Eventually, we could hear the crowd getting rowdy as the game came to an end. We heard a rumbling of footsteps, and I worried people were heading towards the bathrooms, but Lucious assured me differently.

"The elevators are not too far from here, AJ. People are leaving, but let's just stay in here a couple more minutes to make sure."

We stayed in the bathroom and didn't hear any more steps, so Lucious looked through the peephole to see if the coast was clear. Everybody was gone, so he opened the door. As soon as we stepped out, Phoenix was right there waiting. It was like she hid behind the door or something. Lucious proceeded to kneel down, but Phoenix told him not to.

"Lucious, it's okay. You don't have to do that all the time. I know I'm royalty, but you can loosen up a bit with me. Now, can we can talk?" she asked.

While in awe of her natural beauty, I managed to get a few words out to speak to her.

"Phoenix, that was a g-g-great game you had," I said.

"Thanks, but that's not important," said Phoenix.

Lucious then mumbled, "But you didn't even...."

Before he could finish his sentence, I gave him a light jab to the shoulder and he went quiet.

Phoenix continued, "AJ, let me tell you what's going on here. As you probably figured out, my name is Phoenix, and I am Madam Serenity's daughter. Everybody refers to me as the princess, but you can just call me Phoenix. I mean, it's cool and all to have this attention and gratitude shown towards me, but I'm just a 17-year-old kid trying to have fun sometimes."

She then began to tell me who I was and what I was actually doing there.

"AJ, you and Lucious come with me. Nicolas, Sebastian, I'll see you tomorrow," said Phoenix.

Nicolas and Sebastian took off down one of the elevators as Lucious and I went down another one of the 100 elevators on the tenth floor. We exited on the first floor and were met by a bunch of security, the thousands of people who attended the game, and even more people standing by the exit door.

Phoenix was really royalty, and security guards escorted the three of us to the black flying cars with flashing lights. Cameras appeared in her face and, surprisingly, cameras were flashing in my face too! All I heard was "AJ, how does it feel to be the chosen one?" and "As Insecurity has her sights set on universal domination, will you save all Elisians and humans from her mass destruction?"

Chosen one? Me, the chosen one? I was totally confused and didn't understand what was going on. Was this why I was here? Was I some kind of savior of the planet that was fairly new to me? At the moment, I had no more time to dwell on what was going on as I was pushed into one of the flying cars by Lucious and Phoenix's chauffeur.

Phoenix and Lucious hopped in and we were off. We glided through the inner city of Elise, and within seconds, we were traveling miles and miles at high speeds through the countryside. I had thought that Elise was only an upscale high-tech super city of a planet and that it wasn't something else, but I was wrong. I could see the sky clearly; there were streams, trees, and grass everywhere, and outside of this world's flying cars, robots, and technology, there was a resemblance of Elise to Earth.

"May I ask exactly where we're going?" I asked.

Lucious then turned to me and punched my shoulder. He whispered, "AJ, right now is not the time to ask questions."

"Lucious, it's okay; take it easy on him," said Phoenix. "We're going to my home. My parents—Madam Serenity, who you've seen already, and Sir Concord, who you'll meet soon—want to see you."

I couldn't believe it. Elisian royalty wanted to speak to me! In my mind, I prepared myself for what I was going to say to them. *Hello, Madam Serenity and Sir Concord. My name's AJ, and I have no clue why I'm here.*

I turned over my shoulder and Lucious was staring at me once again, but he didn't hit me this time. Instead, he said, "Whatever you're thinking about saying to them, just don't say anything at all."

"How did you...." I began, but before I could finish, Lucious said, "I can just tell."

Eventually, we came up to a huge gate manned by a robot like Jax who hit the access button to let us go through. Then, we drove up a hill to get to Phoenix's house. While on the incline, I could see the huge futuristic architectural masterpiece of a home that Phoenix lived in, and honestly, it was as big—if not bigger—than the entire county of Westchester. And a million-plus people live in Westchester!

I looked at Phoenix and said, "Phoenix, how do you live in a place like this? There have to be like a thousand rooms in this place."

She responded, "There probably are, but I don't really live here that much."

"Wait, so where else do you live?" I asked.

"On Earth, silly! I travel back and forth through my portal for the last eight hours of every day. My parents used to do the same, but now they spend more time on Elise. I've only been able to see them on Earth two days out of the week for the past month."

"Okay, so where on Earth do you live?"

"I live in Hillsborough, California. It's a small town in the Bay Area. It's really nice out there."

"I've never been to California, but I've always wanted to go there."

The two of us finished chatting, and we pulled up to the front of the house. I was so astonished at how big it was that I didn't know what else to say.

The chauffeur landed the vehicle. The car's doors opened, and we exited and went to the front door. Phoenix rang the doorbell, and it scanned her entire body to grant access into the house. The huge doors opened, and Madam Serenity and Sir Concord were waiting for us. Seeing them in person was more intense and nerve-racking than ever.

"Welcome to our home, AJ! Glad you could make it," said Sir Concord.

"This is perfect timing," said Madam Serenity.

All of a sudden, Phoenix said, "Oh my goodness, I can't take it anymore. Can I just tell him?"

I thought, *Oh shit, she's about to say something serious.*

She then looked at me and said, "As the Elisian prophecy states, you are the chosen one. You're our cornerstone to defeating Insecurity and stopping her from taking over not only Elise but Planet Earth as well."

It all made sense at that point, from the game to the paparazzi; I now realized that this 16-year-old skinny nerd from Westchester was magically chosen to save not only the planet I'd known for a few hours but a planet that I'd spent my whole life living on. But what I wanted to know was how and why me?

"Mom, Dad, can I go take a shower now? We just came back from hooping not too long ago, and I'm sweating," said Phoenix.

"Well, before you do that, sweetheart, AJ needs some explaining of what's in store for him. Why don't you take him to the basement where he can see for himself and get a better understanding," said Madam Serenity.

"Okay. Fine. C'mon, AJ; let's make this quick," said Phoenix.

She yanked my arm and dragged me down what looked like a never-ending hallway while Lucious stayed back with

Madam Serenity and Sir Concord. We finally reached some stairs and went on the decline to the basement. When we arrived, there were a bunch of books surrounding foreign gadgets that suited how whacky and technologically advanced the planet was.

We then took off to a big room with a desk in the basement that contained several pictures of different people on the wall. I asked Phoenix who all those people were.

She told me, "Those people are all of my ancestors who have once lived on this planet. Some of them are still alive, but they reside on Earth."

"Do you keep in touch with some of them?" I asked.

"No, not really. To be honest, I'm not really close with my family," said Phoenix.

As we kept walking through the room to stare at more pictures, I had to ask Phoenix another question.

"So, Phoenix, since a lot of Elisians live on Earth as well, does that mean we're...."

Before I could finish, she cut me off and said, "Aliens? Yeah. Since we belong to another planet, I guess you can say that, but just not the kind you're thinking of."

I flipped out! For most of my younger years, I was always afraid of aliens and superhumans, and even though I wasn't green with huge eyes and antennas popping out of my head, it was pretty weird.

"Relax, AJ; there's no need to flip out. Yeah, we might be aliens, but we look just like humans, breathe like them, eat like them, and do the most basic life functions just like them. For instance, I go to high school just like you do and just like the humans do. I have friends, gossip, play sports, and do pretty much anything like them. We just have more intellectual power than them, among other things. But, AJ, don't think too much of it now. Trust me," she said.

Phoenix grabbed a huge book from the desk and opened it up. My eyes glistened like Plankton looking at the Krabby

Patty secret formula as an imaginary light reflected into them.

"This right here is why you're the chosen one," she said. "Here is your family lineage going back many years from your father's side. Your dad doesn't know it, but he's Elisian as well. Your eldest relative originated from this planet and migrated to Earth to create your family lineage. At one point in time, your eldest relative, James Hendrix, saved this very planet's existence."

I asked Phoenix, "How did he save Elise?"

She lifted her hand up and waved it in a circular motion. A bunch of gadgets appeared as Phoenix recreated an illusion of the event for me. All I saw was a man in a rocket go full force into an incoming meteor, and then the worst of the worst happened.

"See, our security intelligence detected a foreign object approaching our planet a few days prior to that day, and Elisians were ill-prepared. Your great grandfather, times a million, volunteered to be a sacrificial lamb in a sense. They developed the only thing that could possibly be developed in a three-day time span to throw the meteor off its course, which was a power rocket. James volunteered to fly the rocket, knowing there was a slim chance of making it back. When they released the rocket when the meteor approached the atmosphere, the two collided, causing the meteor and the rocket to disperse. Elise was then safe, but James didn't make it back," said Phoenix.

The whole illusion was intense to watch and to be honest, I was holding back some tears. That was my family! James risked his life for the betterment of his people and his home, and to know that he was related to me was upsetting to see him pass. Still, it gave me insight into how brave, courageous, and considerate he was.

Phoenix went on to say, "Because of that day, in the Elisian prophecy, it is now known that every first Hendrix child born in each century is the designated chosen one and has the responsibility of leading the defense of this planet any time a foreign security threat approaches Elise."

It all made sense to me at this point. It was destiny for me to be the man! Well, not the man-man—that was Sir Concord—but I was the second man! I finally had a better understanding of why I was here, and I felt a little anxious and nervous but also ready for the challenge. There really wasn't any way out of this, so I had to step up.

We then took off back up the steps, and Phoenix went her separate way to the shower as Lucious called my name and I ran towards him.

"So, now you know, AJ," said Lucious.

I realized my actions at the game could've cost Lucious a huge opportunity as he was the mentor to one of the biggest public figures on the planet, which was me!

"Hey, Lucious, I'm so sorry about earlier. If I had known, I wouldn't have run off like that without you, and you know I don't want you to be in serious trouble with royalty."

My heart started to beat real fast all of a sudden. I began to get nervous and sweaty, and then I started pacing back and forth. My anxiety was kicking my ass and Lucious could see it. He looked startled by the way I was acting and instantly checked on me.

"Oh my gosh, AJ. What's wrong?" asked Lucious.

"Lucious, to be honest, I got the whole breakdown, you know, and I thought I was fine, but I'm starting to feel the pressure," I told him.

"You know what, AJ? Let's go outside for a bit so you can get some fresh air; you definitely need it," he said.

We walked towards the door and Sir Concord appeared from a distance and said, "AJ, Lucious, our chef has prepared dinner for everyone, and we'd love for you two to join us whenever you're ready."

"We'd love to, Sir Concord. We'll be there in just a moment. We just need a minute outside," said Lucious.

"Okay, great. Somebody will buzz you back in, and we'll be waiting in the dining room," said Sir Concord.

Lucious and I took off outside and I confessed to him more about my worries and fears.

"Lucious, what if Insecurity is too strong of a force? What if she's able to tear me down? What if I DIE!!? What if I don't ever see my family again? What if I'm not ready for this, Lucious? I think I want to go back home now."

"AJ, take deep breaths! You have time. You'll be training to fight against her, and you won't be alone. You have me, Madam Serenity, Sir Concord, Phoenix, and the whole Planet Elise behind you. For right now, take the time to get comfortable, and focus on eating a nice meal with the royals. This task is far different than what James sacrificed his life for—no disrespect. You're not only here to defend Elise but to protect Earth from her Insecurity's willpower as well," said Lucious.

"Lucious, can I at least do one thing when I get back home?" I asked.

Lucious responded, "What is it, AJ?"

"Can I tell my family what happened today?"

He said, "Well, they might think you're a madman, but whenever you feel like it is the right time to bring it up to them, you can do so."

I normally told my family everything, and at first, my gut feeling was that I was going to tell them right when I got back home, but I had to think again, and Lucious was probably right.

"Well, AJ, would you like to go eat some delicious food now? I'm kinda hungry, you know," said Lucious.

I agreed and we got buzzed back into the palace. One of the robots escorted us to a huge dining room with a marble table in the middle and the three royals sitting there waiting for us.

My eyes locked onto Phoenix, and she looked absolutely stunning, like she was attending the Met Gala or something.

I started to drool a little as I lusted over this beautiful girl. Lucious saw me, closed my jaw and told me to tighten up. I looked over to Sir Concord and Madam Serenity, and they were stunting as well in high-class fabrics.

"Lucious, AJ, come sit," said Madam Serenity.

Feeling a bit out of place, I spoke for us and told the royals, "We'll sit, but just being honest Madam, Lucious and I feel a little underdressed for this occasion."

"Well, that's not a problem. Jax, fix these two up properly, please," said Madam Serenity.

With a snap of her fingers, two robots were behind us. They grabbed and spun the two of us like twisting tornadoes. We finally stopped spinning, and the robots displayed a mirror in front of us.

We were in flashy tuxedos and sparkly loafers. At that moment, I felt like a million bucks, and I know Lucious did as well.

"There we go! How's that look for you two?" asked Sir Concord.

I looked at Lucious, smiling, and Lucious looked at me, smiling, and at the same time, the two of us said, "Fantastic!"

"Well, that's great. Let's enjoy dinner now," said Phoenix.

There was an empty seat next to her, and of course I was going to sit there. I wanted to get to know her more, not just because I thought she was the most beautiful girl that had ever existed but because she seemed like a great person to talk to. The only problem was that I was horrible at chatting to females in that kind of way. I'd never really had the experience, and the fear of embarrassment always haunted me.

I sat down next to Phoenix as Lucious sat across from me, and Sir Concord and Madam Serenity sat on both ends of the table that was big enough for ten people. The royals then invited the robots to sit in on dinner with us, and I thought that was really nice of them. Even though the robots work for them, the royals treat them more like family than just employees. We had lobster mac 'n' cheese for dinner and it looked amazing as the robots plated our food before they sat down. While the food was being placed on our plates, I had to come up with something to talk about with Phoenix.

"Phoenix, how's your life in the Bay Area?"

"It's alright, I guess. Like I told you before, my parents aren't on Earth most of the time, and when they are, they're too busy working at the headquarters of their large tech company, LyveWire, so I spend most of my time at home alone with the nanny."

"Wait, your parents own LyveWire?"

"Yeah, they do."

"That's like the biggest tech company in America. Your parents are the ones who made my gaming console."

"I guess you can say that, AJ."

"Well, you must be pretty well off then," I said.

"I'll say, AJ. I am in a very blessed situation, but money isn't everything. There are plenty other things I would like to have over the money, but let's not get into that," said Phoenix.

"Okay, okay. My bad. Let me change the subject. What do you do for fun?" I asked.

She paused to take a bite out of her food and then responded, "I play video games, basketball, and I go to parties."

"You mean like birthday parties?" I asked.

She responded, "No, I go to house parties. They're way more fun than b-day parties that parents set up. Plus, my nanny doesn't know about them because she's always on her phone with her boyfriend, so I just sneak out."

I had never been to a house party before, so I asked Phoenix what they were like. "Hey, Phoenix, what goes down at these house parties?"

"You've seriously never been to one before?" Phoenix asked me.

I told her that I hadn't, and she looked at me and laughed.

"AJ, you really need to go out more. I might just have to bring you out to a party one day. Anyway, I'll tell you this but don't want to be too loud because I can't have my parents overhearing this kinda stuff, so lean over a bit," she said.

I leaned over and she whispered in my ear everything!

"Beer, really? That's the stuff my pops drinks when his buddies come over to watch the Knicks on Sunday. They drink that stuff at house parties?" I asked.

"Yeah, AJ, but it's not just that. There's loud music, dancing and just an overall good time, and to be honest, I love it compared to the life I have here. Don't get me wrong, everyone on Elise are nice, genuine people, but it's not as exciting as you think compared to Earth."

"How so, Phoenix? You're the princess of an entire planet!" I said.

"When you say it like that, you think it is exciting, but it really isn't," said Phoenix. She continued, "I only get two hours to have fun while the other six hours I'm stuck in this castle following my mother and father around since I'm next in line for the throne. I love my parents, but I feel like they should let me have more time to be a teenager; you know what I'm saying?"

Sir Concord suddenly called my name and I sat up immediately. I answered, "Yes, Sir Concord?"

"I hope you're enjoying your time so far on Planet Elise," he said.

I responded, "I am truly enjoying my time here."

"Well, that's great, but you know that this is an extremely important role you're playing. The fate of all Elisians and humans on Earth is in our hands as royalty, but it's in yours as well," he said.

"I understand the challenge, Sir Concord. Whatever it takes, I'll make sure Insecurity doesn't ruin what you have going on here and on Earth," I said.

Being the chosen one and having all this pressure on me, I wanted to know more about Insecurity, why people on this planet were so afraid of her and what she could do. I knew she had been on the planet before, and I knew it wasn't pretty, but I clearly needed to know more about my opponent to better prepare myself.

I asked the royals, "If you don't mind me asking, can I know more about Insecurity?"

My question created an awkward silence across the entire dining room, and even the Jax robots stopped chattering. I figured that my question was a sensitive subject and assumed it wasn't going to be answered until Phoenix spoke up.

"Insecurity is my evil auntie. She lives on Planet Iniquitous with all the other demons, and it's about 100,000 miles away from here."

I asked her, "How long does that take to get here?"

She responded, "It's like an hour and thirty minutes in galaxy time—not as far as it seems. I've never met my grandma, but I've heard Dad talk about her. I've heard my dad call my grandma unfaithful—"

Madam Serenity cut Phoenix off and said, "Phoenix! Please don't say what you're about to say."

"Serenity, it's fine," said Sir Concord. He continued, "Insecurity is my half-sister. My mother was with my father, Sir Concord Sr., for a while until she felt she was not as important to him as the people of Elise were. My father was head of the security task force for Elise so his job was to always protect the people. Anyways, my mother wasn't an Elisian —my father traveled through the planet portal and met her on Earth—but he exposed her to this life on Elise. On Earth, she would tell my father she was going to visit her sick mother from time to time, but she was cheating on him with Knave, who was the king of Planet Iniquitous, and had Insecurity with him. Did she know he was an evil king from outer space? No, and she never found out. She passed away years later; my father raised me on his own, and Knave raised that evil witch on his own."

I looked at his face and could see that the subject of Insecurity—and the name Insecurity alone—was painful for him to hear.

"Knave destroyed our security force, entered Elise, and infected my father with the odious virus," said Sir Concord. "I was only sixteen when it happened."

I asked the royals, "What is the odious virus?"

Madam Serenity said, "The odious virus stems from the odious serum created by Knave. It completely eliminates an individual's capacity to have any physiological or behavioral response to positive emotions like happiness and love and enacts negative emotions such as hate, anger, and jealousy. The virus then makes the infected evil and turns them into demons, slowly deteriorating and killing their body over time."

"Well, he and his daughter have something in common. They're both cowards who make viruses to destroy planets because they can't do it themselves," I said.

Sir Concord continued to speak, "My father was at a low point mentally when he found out my mother was cheating, and the virus exposed his weakness. When my father had the virus, we had no choice but to lock him in a chamber so he wouldn't infect others on the planet. He would constantly scream vile things and punch the plexiglass. The virus then took over and he turned into a demonic state.

"I had to step up as commander in chief and then eventually as king since he was unable to serve. We didn't have the technology or a counter serum to combat the odious virus. Luckily, my father miraculously recovered from it, but he was never the same. We used his antibodies to make a counter serum and suppress the virus. Honestly, watching him deteriorate in front of my eyes was the most heartbreaking thing ever, and it hurt him so much that he gave up his life on Elise to reside fully on Earth. He lives a few blocks away from us, but he's in assisted living because of the effects of the odious virus."

Phoenix jumped in and said, "My dad loved my Pop Pop dearly. The two of them were best friends, but since he gave up his life on Elise, if it wasn't for my mother, he'd have nobody to turn to."

I saw tears coming out of Sir Concord's eyes as a mix of distress, pain, and fatigue appeared on his face. He shared so much of his family's life story with me and it hit hard. This family had been through tough times because of evil, cold-hearted individuals that thrived off negativity for validation.

"I think it's best if we steer this conversation in a positive manner or just focus on this wonderful meal!" said Lucious.

Everyone agreed and we continued to enjoy the food and conversation. The royals asked about my family, my life in New York, and school, and it was a great couple of hours. We finished dinner and all got up from the table. As I was leaving, the alarm on the glasses started to ring. I wasn't wearing them but remembered I had put them in my pocket. That was my calling to return home, and I looked around and the royals' alarms were ringing as well.

They escorted us out of their home, but before we could exit the door, Sir Concord said to me, "AJ, I hope you enjoyed your time at our residence as you're always welcome here. In the meantime, we are going to have you train to prepare for the war against Insecurity, and that starts tomorrow. Phoenix will be there to train alongside you, and I hope you tell your family at some point about your little secret."

I looked at Lucious and whispered in his ear, "How long do I have to train for?"

He said to me, "The security task force estimated Insecurity's attack to be anywhere from three months to maybe three years from now."

"Three years? That's a long time!" I said.

Lucious cleared his throat and tapped me on the shoulder. I looked back at Sir Concord and he was awaiting my response.

"My apologies, Sir Concord. I can assure you that I am determined to be the best I can be for this planet, and I will for sure tell my family about this wonderful place when the time is right," I said.

"Well, that's great!" he responded.

"We will see you tomorrow!" said Madam Serenity.

"See you soon, AJ," said Phoenix.

I smiled and Lucious and I walked out the door as the royals waved goodbye. We walked down the steps and turned to each other.

"Same thing tomorrow, Chosen One?" asked Lucious.

I responded back, "You already know, Lucious. See you in the next 24."

The two of us dapped each other up and I hit the exit button. Lucious disappeared, and I started spinning back in the portal, flipping over and over and over again. At the end of the portal, I saw my room getting closer and closer until boom! I flew out and hit my head on the bed frame, knocking out cold.

The next thing I knew, my mother was looking over me with a mean mug on her face. "AJ, what are you doing on the floor? How come you always end up falling while you sleep?" she asked. I stuttered while regaining consciousness and she said, "No time for explaining. You need to get ready for school. Go take a shower and put on some clothes."

She left my room as I took a shower and got ready for school, but to be honest, all that was on my mind was the huge task I had at hand. I had a foreign planet and a huge world to protect from evil, and that whole journey officially began.

CHAPTER 5
STRAIGHT TO BUSINESS

For the next few hours, my day was dry. It was a normal school day consisting of logging onto my computer, attending classes, and turning in homework assignments. Throughout the majority of the day, all I thought about was my first training session on Elise. To be truthful, I was really, really nervous—excited but nervous. I didn't know what to expect, I didn't know how I might perform, and I didn't want to disappoint Lucious and the royals. Plus, training wasn't the only thing I was worried about. I still had to tell my family about traveling to an alternate world with flying cars, being a chosen warrior to save the universe, and belonging to an alien bloodline. To a normal person, all of that would sound crazy—and make me look crazy to them—which made me think I wasn't quite ready to tell them.

A couple meals and a few TV shows later, it was nighttime. Everyone in the house went to sleep, but I stayed up and waited for the portal. After ten minutes, the portal appeared, and it was time! I jumped through and started spinning uncontrollably again. Finally, I reached the end of the portal and landed hard on the ground. When I looked up, Lucious was smiling down at me.

"Ready for your training, Chosen One?" he asked.

I got up and realized I hadn't come through the same entrance as before. There were trees, grass, and a blue sky. I turned around and saw a huge gate and realized I was at the royals' residence.

I said, "You know what? I'm a little nervous, but I'm ready. Let's do this, Lucious!"

"Oh, yeah! Let's go ring the bell," said Lucious.

We went past the gate and rang the doorbell. It scanned the two of us and then granted us access. Waiting for us at the door was Sir Concord in a pretty cool jumpsuit, kind of like what secret agents in movies wear.

"Lucious, AJ, welcome back! AJ, I hope you're ready for your first day of training; it's a very important one," he said.

"Let's do this!" I said.

"I love the energy, AJ! Let's get to it then," said Sir Concord.

We then walked through many major hallways in the house, past several robots walking by. I was confused about where he was taking us since I'd seen so little of the house. I looked at Lucious to see if he knew.

He looked back at me and whispered, "I'm in the same boat as you, AJ. It's your first time training, and it's my first time watching, so I'm as lost as you are."

"We're heading towards the backyard, gentlemen, in case you were wondering. Our house is a little high up, so we have to take the elevators to get to the backyard," said Sir Concord. "Madam Serenity is in her office, and Phoenix is waiting for us outside and will be joining you in training, AJ."

Phoenix. Hearing that name gave me real-life heart eyes and made me all bubbly inside. I could just imagine her in an amazing dress, hair all curly with fine jewelry on, walking down the steps of her New York City apartment as I waited for her in our fancy limo to take us to a romantic dinner date at a five-star restaurant. I pictured it like a scene out of a modern romance movie.

We reached the set of elevators at the end of the hall and entered the middle one. It descended at an immense speed, and I got pushed back and stuck to its wall like a fly in a spiderweb. While stuck, I looked at Lucious and Sir Concord, shocked that the two of them were standing straight with no problem. The two of them looked at each other, then looked at me and began to laugh. The elevator stopped and I fell from the wall onto the floor. The door opened up as Lucious and Sir Concord helped me off the floor.

When we got out, my jaw dropped. I couldn't even fathom what I was seeing! It was like a science lab and training camp mixed together. Thousands and thousands of Elisians and robots were walking around everywhere. There were even huge test tubes with people in them while kids and adults in lab coats and with clipboards examined them. I looked a little to my left and saw thousands of flying cars, but they were different than the normal ones. They had two launchers, one on the passenger side and one on the driver's side, and a third smaller launcher in the front. They resembled drones but super magnified and lethal.

I looked to Sir Concord and said, "Your Majesty, if you don't mind me asking, did you bring the entire planet to your backyard?"

He responded, "Yes, AJ, pretty much. To be fair, I had to create an environment as realistic as possible for you and the rest of the planet to prepare for future battles. Preparation builds our skills and character."

"So, what will I be doing first, Sir Concord?" I asked.

He said, "You will be working in the combat training chambers first, into which I will escort you and Lucious. Phoenix is already in there training, so you'll see her. After that, Lucious will escort you to the aircraft training station and then the recovery station."

"You mean those weird test tube things with all the wires and stuff?" I asked.

"Yes, AJ, the 'weird test tube things,'" said Sir Concord. "Those stations are where we analyze your vitals to make sure you're in top-tier shape to fight against Insecurity."

All of this news was astonishing to me. Elisians were truly amazing individuals with the sole intention of making the universe a better place for existence, and I couldn't be any prouder to be one.

Lucious then said, "With all of this new information, AJ, you have to act like you know nothing at all when you go back through the portal; don't tell anybody!"

"What about my family?" I asked.

Sir Concord laughed aggressively with the biggest smile on his face. He said to me, "We've already got that covered. We've seen how self-conscious and worrisome you appear when in the presence of others. It was obvious at the dinner table the other day. We also noticed that you lose focus when you have time on your hands, but we'll work on that, for sure."

My cheeks turned red as I smiled awkwardly in embarrassment. "I guess it was pretty obvious, wasn't it?" I asked.

Sir Concord smiled again and then snapped his fingers. All of a sudden, I heard screaming from a far distance, then it got closer and closer and closer. I looked up, and two holes appeared in the sky. They were two portals with two dudes descending, yelling at the top of their lungs on the way down. I tried to take a closer look and felt like I recognized them. Then, I heard a loud voice behind me scream, "Junior! You better tell me what the hell is going on right now!"

I turned around. I would recognize that voice anywhere. Nobody ever called me Junior but one person. My mother, Lil Man and Madam Serenity were walking over from the elevators! I stood there in shock. My body couldn't move, my lips felt vacuum-sealed, my eyelids were stretched wide open, and all of a sudden, boom! Everything went black for about a minute. As I regained consciousness, all I could hear was muffled chatter around me. I tried to get up, but for some reason, I couldn't. I realized someone's back was turned to my face.

Struggling to rise, I flipped to my right side, and their body fell over towards the left. As I finally got up, I started to hear things more clearly. My mother still sounded confused, my little brother was crying, and as I saw my dad get up from the ground, he went over to where my mother and Lil Man were with Madam Serenity. The royals had brought my family here, but I felt one more person was missing.

I felt a tap on my shoulder, and as I turned around, he was in my face. "Hey, AJ! My fault; did I get you there?" asked Kevin, laughing.

"Yes, you did, and it wasn't fucking funny," I said.

"Well, that guy over there thinks otherwise," said Kevin. He pointed his finger to my left and Lucious stood there laughing so hard he was bent over and gasping for air. Sir Concord gave him a hard tap on his shoulder and told him to cut it out. He stopped and stood straight up. My mom, baby bro, dad, and Madam Serenity approached, and my mother got in my face.

"Junior, you better tell me what's going on here. Your father and I woke up to your little brother crying in the middle of the night in his room, wondering what the hell had him up so late at night. We turned our heads and got sucked into some weird circle thing in the closet. You know your father and I like to get our beauty sleep."

Puzzled and struggling to find words to say, I just began to stutter, "I...I...I...I don't know what to say."

Kevin blurted out, "You guys didn't jump through it?" I turned to Kevin and he whispered, "What? Muhfucka, you know if you saw some cool shit glowing from your closet, you finna jump through that shit and check it out."

I couldn't argue because I did the same exact thing to get here. I sighed as he continued, "I was trying to see if that shit would take me to Mars, but this is way better."

Sir Concord stepped in. "Everyone, calm down. I will explain to you and the rest of your family, Mrs. Hendrix, what is going on here. For now, my wife and I will take you around the estate while your son goes off to his combat training. Lucious, take AJ on his way."

"Combat what? Somebody better tell me something!" said my mom. My father held her hand as they went off.

As Kevin trotted off with the rest of my family, he saw one of the combat drones and said, "Whoa! I want to drive one of those!"

Sir Concord stopped him in his tracks and picked him up to catch up with everybody else.

"Well, that was awk-warrrrrd!" said Lucious.

"Yeah, very," I responded.

Lucious and I then went on our way to learn alien karate and how to use cool-looking laser guns. We arrived at the combat training station and entered the door. There were a bunch of people in large groups doing synchronized flips and air punches as well as shooting virtual representations of Iniquitans with laser guns. I peeked in a little further and there she was, looking more stunning than ever. I never imagined a female could look so amazing while kicking ass until now. I knew now that if someone tried to break into the house, I wouldn't be fighting by myself.

Lucious and I headed over towards her as her training session came to an end. We finally reached her and she smiled.

"AJ, nice to see you here. Are you ready?" Phoenix asked.

I told her that I was ready for whatever. She said, "Cool! I just finished my training, but I have nothing else better to do, so I'll join you."

When she said that, it made me a little nervous. Because I had a romantic love interest in her, even though she didn't know it yet, I knew I would have a hard time focusing. However, I didn't want to be the chosen one and not possess the skills and attributes needed.

"Let's not dilly dally; let's get straight to business. The instructor and everybody else is waiting for you, AJ," said Lucious.

All of the instructors were robots and taught kids my age—or maybe even older—how to properly fight in the heat of battle. We got to the practice battlefield and my instructor greeted me, but in a very weird way. He stepped towards me, and all of the other hundred students stood behind him, waiting to shake my hand.

The instructor said to me, "Welcome, Chosen One! As instructed by Sir Concord, I will be your teacher and these will be your classmates. We're all excited to meet you and get to work with you, and I hope you are as well."

The instructor then shook my hand and the kids followed. One by one, each student came up to me, bowed their heads, and shook my hand. It felt weird. I wasn't their elder or anything; I was a teen just like the rest of them. After everyone shook my hand, we all lined up in front of the instructor.

With Phoenix by my side and Lucious watching, it was officially time. The instructor pressed a button on his wrist, and a virtual battlefield popped out and laser guns appeared in our hands. I could see everyone's faces, even Phoenix's, and their intense looks let me know they were ready. The practice enemies were all spread out, and the instructor gave us our instructions.

"In this practice battle, you all have to eliminate the enemies within three minutes; each individual has to at least eliminate twenty enemies before time runs out. The red button on your weapons is your normal ammunition. The green button is your explosive ammunition, but keep in mind that it isn't unlimited, so choose wisely. Also, be aware of and utilize your surroundings. Overall, you are all a family out there, and family sticks together. If one of your members is down, you pick them right up. We ride for each other, and we die for each other."

All of a sudden, there was a loud countdown. "Five, four, three, two, one!"

Everyone took off running. We all charged the battlefield, dodging lasers and explosives while shooting them back. I could see Phoenix thriving in her element, as well as the others, while I was out there like a chicken with its head cut off. I was running on pure adrenaline and had no awareness of my surroundings. My fear came to light as I was truly looking bad. I knew that people saw me looking lost out there, but suddenly things turned for the better.

I got hit by a laser, and everything clicked. That pain from that laser was the same pain that I felt from all those insecurities I had to deal with at school, the same pain I felt by being judged and bullied, the same pain I felt from rejection, and the same pain I felt dealing with my addiction. I turned that pain into rage and went on a rampage. One enemy to another went down like flies as I eliminated them with my laser shots. I was going crazy, and as the three minutes ended, I realized I was on top of the performance leaderboard and even surpassed Phoenix! I guess my rage brought out the best of my combat abilities, which was going to be helpful when it came down to the real thing.

We regrouped, and all of my peers congratulated me. It went from loud claps and cheers to a lot of "Good job, Chosen One!" and "Awesome job, Chosen One!". Then, finally, the affirmation I was looking for came from my future wife.

Phoenix walked up to me and said, "AJ, that was amazing what you did out there! What got into you?"

I responded, "I really don't know, Phoenix."

"Well, whatever it is, keep doing what you're doing," she said.

"Thanks, my love," I replied.

She looked at me crazy. "Look, AJ, I like you. I think you're a very unique kind of guy, and you really impressed all of us today, but I'm not looking for anything romantic right now, and I noticed from the jump your huge crush on me," she said.

My puppy eyes of joy turned into sad eyes as I prepared for rejection. "Oh, um, okay. Sorry for my forward comment earlier," I said.

She looked at me and smiled. "It's alright. It's just that, for one, we're a year apart, and two, I'm just not ready. But, it doesn't mean I'm not open to it in the future," said Phoenix.

I switched emotions once again and smiled as I felt the sense of opportunity. "Never say never?" I asked.

She responded, "Never say never."

I realized I had been rejected, but it wasn't as bad as I'd always feared. She turned me down but not all the way, so my feelings weren't hurt.

We rejoined Lucious, and the three of us moved onto the second training session—where I learned how to fly and shoot the lasers on the drones, which was amazing—and then onto the rest station where the scientists put me in the capsule.

The whole training experience was amazing, and I honestly couldn't wait to do it again. As training came to an end, everyone started to file out while Lucious, Phoenix and I went back inside the house to see what was going on with my parents. We went up the elevator and walked down the hallway to laughter and chatter from the dining area. We entered the dining room, and there was my family enjoying a nice meal while chopping it up with the royals.

My father looked at me while enjoying his food and said, "Son, these nice, thoughtful and generous people have explained to us why you're here and what's going on."

My mother chimed in, "Yes, Junior, and I'm telling you now, as your mother, you better be doing your best out there training to save this damn universe!"

Then there came my brother sitting next to Lil Man with a turkey leg in his mouth. "Yeah, muhfucka. You better not fuck this shit up, along with these other people, cuz I ain't ready to die yet."

My mother screamed across the table and said, "Kevin, watch your mouth! We're guests here, so be respectful."

"That's okay, Mrs. Hendrix. Besides, we're all one family here, and because you have now been informed of the situation, we've cleaned up rooms in the house for all of you to enjoy!" said Sir Concord. He continued, "Also, here are your glasses; they are your way in and out of this world. AJ can explain more to you."

My family looked confused, but they carried on with their meal. Lucious, Phoenix and I sat down with the rest of them at the table and enjoyed a chat as a family.

Madam Serenity tapped her glass and everyone went quiet. She went on to speak. "Phoenix, my child, if I'm not mistaken, isn't your formal in a few months?"

"You mean prom, Mother, and yes it is. Why do you ask?" asked Phoenix.

"Well, I haven't heard of you mentioning a date escorting you to the dance," responded Madam Serenity.

For a moment, I was confused. I thought, *How can she have a school dance. Isn't the killer virus still going on?* But then I remembered it was only temporary.

Phoenix said, in an uncomfortable tone, "No, I don't, Mother."

"Well, that's great; AJ can escort you to the dance then," said Sir Concord.

Around the table were a bunch of confused and shocked faces, including mine.

All of a sudden, Kevin blurted out, "Yessir, my boy! My brother is going to the prom, you heard!"

That's why I loved Kevin. Not only was he super funny, but he was unapologetically himself no matter where he was.

My mom went on to speak. "Concord, Serenity, I know that just meeting you two, we've clicked and got along, but I don't think sending my son over to California to stay with a family we don't know that well is a good idea."

"You all are welcome to join us at our estate in Hillsborough. It'll give our families some time to get to know each other," said Madam Serenity.

"We'll even send the private plane to JFK for you all to take over," said Sir Concord.

My mother said, "Oh, I don't know," but before she continued, my father interrupted her and said, "The dance is in June, correct?"

"That's right!" said Madam Serenity.

My father said, "We'll be at JFK. Just send us the time and date."

As usual, Kevin chimed in, "Let's go!"

Then my little brother said, "Yay! Vacation!"

Kevin continued, "AJ, Lil Man, it's up, gang! You know I'm finna be flexing on the gram! We flying private!"

I knew Kevin would be excited, especially by flying on a private jet, because he could flex on his social media page.

Phoenix and I turned to each other, and she said to me, "One, please try not to embarrass yourself or me. And Two, no discussions about Elise whatsoever! Got it?"

Looking a little intimidated, I stared into her eyes and nodded. She said, "Good. Well, I hope you know how to dance," and the conversation ended.

A few hours passed, and it was time to leave once again. The entire day was a weird but eventful experience as my family learned about their alien lineage, enjoyed a nice meal, and planned a free weekend trip to San Francisco while I trained to fight millions of devilish Iniquitans for the sake of the universe's existence.

CHAPTER 6
A DANCE WITH THE DEVIL

For the next few months, things on Earth were great. The killer virus began to dwindle away just like Madam Serenity said it would. My brothers and I went back to school, my parents went back to their jobs, and everything looked amazing. Because things on Earth were doing so much better, I had a lot of time during the day to strictly focus on training, and that was going well. I was still performing at a high level at the training stations, and Kevin was also doing surprisingly well. I guess that *Call of Duty* was paying off pretty heavily for him. Even when it came to the resting station, the doctors said that all of my family members'— including Lil Man's—vitals were extraordinary!

It gave me the utmost confidence that Insecurity and whatever she had cooking up was no match. Time passed by, and I cruised through school with more confidence and pep in my step than ever before. What also helped was that I finally got rid of my braces, grew a couple inches taller and started to look more appealing to the ladies who wouldn't even look my way before. But not only did I only have one woman on my mind, all of that stuff just wasn't that important.

What was important was that the Elisian people and I had the opportunity to save the world from evil and that I wasn't just doing it for the greater good, but I was doing it to make my family proud.

June 15 came around and the school year for me was over, but it was two days before Phoenix's prom. The whole week leading up to it, she would not only talk to me about it during training, but she texted me nonstop about the type of dress she was gonna wear, the color she wanted and how she wanted us to match colors to the tee. It was a little overwhelming, but I liked it. Having the girl that I had the biggest crush on talk to me nonstop felt like we were in a relationship, even though we were just friends.

The next day, it was finally time to hop on the private jet that Phoenix's parents sent over. We all packed a couple bags for the weekend trip and headed down to JFK International Airport, where the jet was waiting for us. When we got to the airport and went through basic security, three large gentlemen in black suits escorted us to the jet. We reached the takeoff spot and my parents looked shocked, like they had seen a ghost, while my two brothers were giddy like they had run off with all of the neighborhood candy on Halloween. We went up the jet's steps with our luggage, and to our surprise, there he was.

"Well, what do you think?" asked Sir Concord.

"Concord, this is absolutely amazing!" said my father.

"I agree," said my mother.

Sir Concord responded, "Well, I'm glad you all like it. In the meantime, put your bags down, sit, and relax as we'll be here for a couple hours. I've also planned out the weekend for us while AJ and Phoenix are at the dance."

"Well, what about the boys?" my mom asked.

"Serenity has that taken care of. The nanny will watch over them, and Serenity invited her nephews over for the boys to have people to hang out with," said Sir Concord.

Kevin then shouted, "When's this jet taking off, man? I'm ready to go!"

Coincidentally, the pilot came out of the cockpit and said, "Ready for takeoff, Mr. Maxwell?"

"Yes, we're all ready," said Sir Concord.

We took off, and for the next couple of hours, it was a relaxing ride. I honestly couldn't say much about how it went because the seats were so comfy that I fell asleep like a baby. When I woke up, we were already at the San Francisco airport. All of us hopped off the jet with our bags and entered a limo waiting to take us to the royal estate. The ride was about half an hour long, but it was annoying as Kevin hit me nonstop on the shoulder in excitement, and even Lil Man chimed in.

"Yo, AJ, I'm not gonna lie, brother. I was creeped out about this new planet/save the world shit, but if we get to do shit like this, I'm with it, man!" said Kevin. He went in and hugged me, and so did Lil Man.

I told them, "Both of you, just be cool and on your best behavior because whatever y'all do is a reflection of us."

"We promise, AJ," said Lil Man.

We reached the top of the hill in the quiet neighborhood, and to no surprise, there was the estate. It basically resembled the home on Elise. There was a big entrance gate and a nice green yard, and I could already picture what the house looked like on the inside. I always wondered how Phoenix, at her age and with all the luxuries life had given her, always remained humble and never let it define who she was. The life she lived is what millions of people like me strove for, but she wasn't the type to gloat about it. She was truly different.

We pulled up to the front of the mansion where Phoenix and Madam Serenity were standing, waiting as per usual to greet us, but there was a third woman there. I guessed that was the nanny. The driver opened the limo doors, and we hopped out, entered the humongous estate and settled our stuff down. Like normal, we gathered around the dining room table for a meal Madam Serenity made.

Madam Serenity started the conversation. "Tomorrow's your big day, honey!"

"I know, Mom," said Phoenix.

"Well, are you excited? You know, this is your prom!"

"Yes, Mom," said Phoenix.

She looked at me and shook her head, letting me know that she wasn't as excited as her mother.

I leaned over and asked her, "Why aren't you excited for your prom?"

"Well, the prom is gonna be nothing compared to tonight," Phoenix whispered.

"What's happening tonight?" I asked.

"I'm taking you to your first house party tonight! My friend Shannon is hosting a big party since her parents are out of town for the weekend, and the whole school's gonna be there!"

I was excited that I was going to my first house party, but I was also nervous because, for one, I'd never snuck out in the middle of the night before, and two, I didn't know how to act or what to do at house parties.

Suddenly, my mother addressed Madam Serenity and Sir Concord. "Serenity, Concord, I can't thank you two enough for welcoming us into your home once again. I just want to ask, what are your plans for us adults on this trip?"

Madam Serenity answered, "We're going to leave Hillsborough and show you and your husband around San Francisco! We'll go out to eat and enjoy all of the touristy things you may see about San Fran on TV. The nanny is going to take the two boys to a few amusement parks and carnivals so they can have some fun, and don't worry, they'll be fine."

My mom and dad said okay, and our families continued to bond for the rest of the night. Finally, it reached 11:30, and we all went to our respective rooms for the night. I stayed up, waiting for Phoenix to knock on the door to tell me the coast was clear. Our plan for sneaking out of the house was for Phoenix to check all the rooms to see if everyone was asleep—if their bedroom doors were locked, it meant they were. Then, she would turn off the outdoor camera system and do a special knock on my door to let me know the coast was clear.

As I waited for Phoenix, I went to the closet and changed into the freshest outfit I had as I was really trying to impress her. Normally, my wardrobe consisted of a button-up shirt, a sweater and some slacks, but I figured I couldn't wear that to the party and look like a square. Instead, I grabbed my fitted jeans, a pink t-shirt, a pair of white canvas sneakers, and, to put everything all together, a dope designer hoodie that I stole from Kevin's closet back home. I looked in the mirror and felt like the flyest dude on Earth, and I knew for sure that Phoenix was gonna dig my outfit.

A few minutes passed, and I heard the special knock on the door. I went over and opened it. Phoenix came in with a beautiful dress, nice curly hair and glowing skin.

While I was being mesmerized by her natural beauty, Phoenix asked, "You ready to go?"

"Yeah, I'm ready," I responded.

"Good, then let's go. The camera systems are shut off, so no one will know we left unless they check our rooms, which I highly doubt. Also, be very quiet going down the steps."

I was kinda disappointed that Phoenix didn't acknowledge my nice outfit, but I didn't let that faze me. We left my room and walked down the stairs quietly to leave out the front door. Phoenix had previously told me that Shannon's house was only a ten-minute walk.

As we reached the bottom of the steps, we slowly crept to the front door. As we opened the door and stepped one foot outside, we suddenly heard, "Where y'all going without me?"

I would recognize that voice anywhere, and I knew it was my brother Kevin. He was in the dark kitchen, eating a sandwich while drinking a Coca-Cola.

"What, I can't pull up to the function with y'all? I know y'all going to a party."

Before I could even say anything, Phoenix chimed in. "Yeah, sure. You can come, but lower your voice. And why are you in my kitchen eating our sandwich meat in the dark?"

"Well, I was hella hungry, and I didn't wanna wake anybody up, so I figured I'd come down, make myself a sandwich and crash on the couch in the living room."

"I guess that makes sense," I said.

"Okay. If you're coming with us, don't you want to change into something else?" Phoenix asked.

"You must be bugged the fuck out, shawty. This right here is a VLONE sweatsuit. I ain't gonna change nothing," said Kevin.

"Okay, my bad," said Phoenix.

My brother is such a hype beast. For a couple years now, he's been running his own sneaker reselling website, and he spends all the money he gets from it on designer shit. From shoes to pants to shirts to socks to even pajamas—if it wasn't designer, it wasn't for Kev. One thing I had to admit, though, was that his fits were fire, which is why I took his hoodie.

Kevin put down the sandwich and soda, joined us at the door and we set off for Shannon's party. Within thirty seconds of us leaving the estate, Kevin noticed I had one of his hoodies on, and he gave me the death stare.

"AJ, is that double Gs I see on that hoodie? I could've sworn I have a hoodie that looks just like that one."

"Okay, Kev, I apologize. I took your hoodie, but I only did it to impress."

Kevin saw me winking and knew I was trying to impress Phoenix.

"Oh, I see. Well, I'm not mad at you, dawg. It actually fits you nice, to be honest. Just don't get it stained, or I'll have to knock you the fuck out," he said.

We continued to walk to the party, and the next nine minutes and thirty seconds consisted of Kevin being loud and jumping up and down.

"I can sense you don't get out much, either," said Phoenix.

"I'm a bag chaser, Phoenix. I ain't got time to go out unless I'm out getting this muhfuckin paper!" said Kevin.

Phoenix looked at Kevin and laughed. "Whatever you say, dude!"

We finally reached Shannon's house; I swear everyone in Hillsborough must be billionaires because her house was just as big as Phoenix's house. The only difference was that the entrance gate was a little smaller. As we got past the entrance, a bunch of people hopped out of cars and entered the huge estate. We entered the party, and it was a crazy sight! Hundreds of people—or maybe even a few thousand—were dancing to loud music with different colored party lights flashing everywhere. I was truly out of my element.

As we walked further into the estate, the three of us heard a voice scream Phoenix's name, and we looked to see where it came from. Suddenly, all three of us saw a girl, short in stature and with curly blonde hair, push through the crowd to get to us. She had two other girls, both a little taller but with straight, dark brown hair, following her.

"Oh my gosh, Phoenix. You made it!"

"Shannon, you're my best friend. You know I couldn't miss your party. Hey Shelby! Hey Lexi!" said Phoenix.

"Hey Phoenix!" the other two girls said simultaneously.

"Well, well, well. Who do we have here?" asked Shannon.

"These are family friends. This is AJ and his brother Kevin," said Phoenix.

"What's good, shawty? You tryna holla at a real go-getter?" said Kevin.

"Um, I was talking about him," said Shannon. She pointed at me and gave me an intimidating look which kinda made me uncomfortable.

"Well, forget you, then. What's going on, Shelby? Lexi? What we doing tonight, ladies?" asked Kevin. He put his arms around the two of them, and they went off to party.

"Well, AJ, why don't I show you around the house?"

"You know what, Shannon? That is a great idea. AJ, I'll meet up with you later," said Phoenix.

Phoenix then split one way, and Shannon grabbed my arm and took me the other way. I was truly pissed because I only went to the party for Phoenix. I wanted this night to be a special moment between us, but that wasn't gonna happen now. Shannon proceeded to drag me through the crowd of people to show me the many different rooms within her home. She took me to her parents' home office, the game room, and the mini movie theater in the basement. While Shannon was showing me around the mini theater, she said she was thirsty, so we headed back upstairs to the party to go to the kitchen. Going through the big crowd once again, we reached the kitchen, where there were a bunch of people sitting on the countertops with red cups and a lot of liquor bottles surrounding them.

"Shannon, cool party, bruh," said one guy.

Then, everyone in the kitchen began to cheer, "Shannon! Shannon! Shannon!"

She started blushing and thanked everyone. "AJ, you want a drink?" she asked.

"Oh, I don't drink that stuff. I'll be okay with just some water, please," I responded.

"Oh, okay. I'll grab a cold water from the fridge."

Suddenly, someone blurted out, "Ha! Pussy! Who brought this bozo here?"

I looked around, and all eyes were on me. Everyone in the kitchen started chiming in by laughing and pointing at me. I felt the laughs get louder and louder with every second that passed, and everybody started getting closer towards me. I began to panic. My heart started to beat really fast, I began to sweat, and I was feeling extremely overwhelmed, so I needed to find a place to isolate myself from the party. I darted out of the kitchen like a mad man, but so many people were crowding the front door that I couldn't leave, so I tried looking for a bathroom.

I'd seen people going up and down the long spiral staircase, so I figured there had to be a bathroom upstairs. I aggressively pushed through the crowd and started running up the steps. When I reached the top of them, I saw an open door in the hallway with the lights on and a girl leaving the room. I ran to the door as fast as I could like Usain Bolt, closed the door, locked it and crawled into a fetal position on the floor.

I was having the worst panic attack ever. I felt like this was it. My last day alive on Earth was being spent lying on a stranger's bathroom floor, and the only thing I could think of to do was close my eyes and hope that it would end, so that's what I did. All I could see was darkness. The music from outside got quieter, my heartbeat slowed down, and I felt like I was sinking through the floor. I went unconscious and truly thought I was dead, but that thought changed rather fast.

Suddenly, I could hear the music getting louder and louder again. I didn't feel like I was sinking through the floor anymore, and I could sense the bathroom light shining on my eyelids. Then, while balled up like an armadillo, I opened my eyes and saw the door handle jiggling. Somebody was picking the lock, trying to get into the bathroom, and any second now, they were gonna see me at my worst.

The door opened, and to my surprise, it was Phoenix and Shannon.

"Oh my gosh! AJ, what's wrong? Are you okay?" asked Phoenix

"How'd you know I was in here?" I asked.

"Well, I saw you running up the steps and figured you were here, so I went and got Phoenix to check on you with me," said Shannon.

"To answer your question, Phoenix, no, I'm not okay. I'm sick and tired of the bullshit: people laughing at me and criticizing me. I'm just tired of it all," I said.

"What are you talking about?" asked Phoenix.

"Just forget it. You won't understand," I responded.

Phoenix looked at Shannon and said, "Can you give us a second?"

"Yeah, of course. I'll be outside," she said.

Shannon left, and it was just the two of us.

"Phoenix, to be honest, you don't have to deal with what I went through. You have it all: the money, huge house, private jet, good looks, friends, all of that. I bet you don't have to worry about being judged at all, while I've spent years of being bullied because of the way I look and the things I say and do. I've never been able to fit in and feel good about myself."

Phoenix sighed and picked me up off the floor. "AJ, look. I get it that people can be mean, and kids around our age, especially, can be assholes, but what you've done is allow your insecurities to stem from what other people think about you. So, you know what you should do?"

"What should I do?" I asked.

She put both hands on my shoulders and stared me in the eyes. "You say fuck 'em, with your head up high, and you keep living your life. Stop caring about what other people think. I may not experience judgment much, but my parents do."

"How so?" I asked.

She responded, "My parents' relationship gets criticized a lot by some people that they know and work with, and my parents have shared with me what their peers say. Because my father is white and my mom is black, they hear from both sides things like 'why her?' or 'why him?' and 'what's so special about them?' My parents know what is meant by that, but they don't care what others think because they love each other, and that's all that matters."

Phoenix didn't stop there as she had something else to say to me. "Also, AJ, I recognize that I am lucky to have the things I have in life, but you've seemed to lose focus of the one thing you have that many people, including myself, don't.

"And what is that exactly?" I asked.

"You have a close relationship with your family. I saw it when they first arrived to Elise and when you all got here, as well. I wish I could get along with my parents like that. The banter, hugs, smiles and laughter you all share is something I want to share with my mom and dad. When they talk to me, it's only about Planet Elise, nothing else. Sometimes, I feel like they care about that planet more than they do their own daughter." Phoenix started to tear up.

I responded, "Wow, Phoenix. My apologies that you feel that way, and I guess you're right. I focused on a lot on things that shouldn't matter much to me, and I lost sight of what really matters, which is my family."

I wiped the tear off her face and gave her a big hug. She smiled and said, "Good! Now let's go find your crazy ass brother and get out of here!"

I agreed, and we left the bathroom to search for Kevin. As we reached the bottom of the steps, the music cut off, and the two of us could hear a loud commotion amongst everyone. We pushed through the crowd and saw a bunch of people in a circle surrounding what must've been a fight. We pushed through to see who it was, and of course, it was Kevin.

He was putting the beats on this one guy so bad that I had to jump in. Phoenix stayed back as I ran in and screamed, "Kevin, stop! Just stop!"

I pulled him off the kid, and Kevin's knuckles were covered in blood.

"You lucky my brother came just in time to save your ass, pussy! Next time you spit on me again, you'll have more than just a broken nose!" my brother screamed at the guy on the floor.

I grabbed his arm and said, "C'mon, Kev. We gotta go now!"

As I dragged him away, he looked back and screamed, "Shelby, I'll call you tomorrow!"

We made our way out the front door with Phoenix and started to walk back to her house.

"Kevin, what the fuck was that?" I asked.

"The muhfucka' had it coming to him."

"What started it, Kevin?" asked Phoenix.

"Long story short, Lexi ditched Shelby and me while we were dancing, so Shelby and I danced together. The bozo I beat up walked by and smacked Shelby on her ass, so I grabbed him by his shirt and said, 'I should beat your ass up right now.' You know what he said to me?"

"What did he say, Kev?" I asked.

"He said 'Well do it then, bitch!' and spit in my face. Then y'all know the rest. Shelby even asked me to be her date to the prom tomorrow, but I think I shouldn't go for that kid's sake."

"I think that's a good idea, Kevin. Another good idea is cleaning up them hands of yours. We don't want our parents knowing you almost beat a kid to death," said Phoenix.

"Fasho, fasho," said Kevin.

Ten minutes later, we were back at the estate. Phoenix pulled out her keys and gently opened the door. We quietly crept inside and went upstairs. Phoenix and I went to our rooms while Kev went to the bathroom to clean the blood off his knuckles. I immediately turned off the lights and jumped in the bed as I knew I was gonna have to get up in a few hours; any amount of sleep that I could get was fine with me.

A few hours later, the sun was reflecting on the blinds in my room, and I woke up to Kevin banging on the bedroom door. "AJ, wake the fuck up! It's 11:30. Breakfast has been ready downstairs for a minute, just to let you know."

I got out of bed and opened the door. "I'm up, Kev. Can you stop now?" I asked.

He looked at me, laughed and went back down the steps. I went to the bathroom to brush my teeth and wash up before I joined everyone for breakfast. Once I finished, I went down the steps to the kitchen to devour a plate of eggs and then went back upstairs to get ready for the big day. I changed out of my pajamas and put my suit on. An hour later, my family knocked on the door and joined me in my room to see my suit.

It was sparkly blue like the ocean and was a suit that would draw the attention of anybody walking by. I could see the joy within my parents' eyes and how excited they were for me.

My dad gave me a hug and said, "Son, you look like a star!"

"Thanks, Dad," I said.

"Oh my, Junior! You're growing up so fast!" said my mother.

All of a sudden, Lil Man ran up to me and gave me a huge hug and wouldn't let go.

"AJ, you look really swaggy, my boy, but you know what you need?" said Kevin.

"Nah, what do I need, Kev?" I asked.

He went into his pocket and pulled out something. "Ice, my boy!" said Kevin.

He had whipped out a nice watch that I had seen my father wear multiple times, and I think my father noticed it too.

"Boy, why do you have my watch?" asked my dad.

"Never mind that; my boy has to get ready for the dance!" said my mom.

Kevin slapped the watch on my wrist, and the ice blinded my eyes. I was finally ready to go, and we went down the steps to wait for Phoenix and her parents.

A few minutes went by, and there she was, walking down with her parents. She was a true princess! She was the dream prom date. Any teen boy around my age would love to be in the spot I was in. Her hair was all shiny, her skin was glowing, and as she got closer, her eyes were even more appealing than usual to stare into. Her dress and shoes were also absolutely sensational! The dress was an ocean blue color with the tiniest sparkles around it that just made it pop. Her shoes were white heels with more VVS diamonds than Drake's OVO chain and reflected light like crazy. She reached the bottom of the steps with her mother and father's arms locked together. Her mother then let go of her arms, and her father followed, smiling as if he was handing his daughter off to me at the altar.

"Well, are you ready to go?" asked Phoenix.

"Yeah, let's do this," I responded.

Sir Concord chimed in. "I know the limo's waiting outside, but Phoenix, I want you to call us once the dance is over and take the limo back to the house; otherwise, have fun, you two!"

"I will, Dad," said Phoenix.

We left out the front door and waved back to our families as we went into the limo to head off to the prom. The school was about twenty minutes away from the house. The ride was pretty silent, with the two of us not even looking at each other until I saw Phoenix reach into her dress out of the corner of my eye and pull out small laser guns.

She caught me staring, and with an angry look on her face, she immediately said, "AJ! What in the actual fuck?"

I responded, "What am I supposed to do, Phoenix? You just pulled two laser guns from your bra. If you saw me pulling two laser guns from my jock, you're telling me you wouldn't be suspicious?"

"Ew, AJ. You're so fucking gross!"

"I know, but that's beside the point. Why did you bring those guns?"

"Well, you never know what can happen, and if a guy tries to get a little creepy on the dance floor, he'll catch this third-degree laser burn."

"You don't need those laser guns for that. I can handle the simple douchebag for you."

Phoenix looked at me and laughed hard.

"What's so funny, Phoenix?"

"Um, have you ever fought someone?" she asked. She saw the confused look on my face as I struggled to find an answer. "That's what I thought. AJ, you might want to take one of these for yourself," she said in a laughing matter.

She handed me the other laser gun, and I shamefully placed it in the back of my pants. To avoid any more embarrassment, I decided to lighten the mood and change the subject. I began to ask Phoenix questions about the dance like, "Are you excited?", "Are we sitting with your friends" and "Do you know how to dance because I don't." All of her responses were a simple "yes," and we finally arrived. A bunch of kids were going up the steps to enter the school as we exited the limo.

Phoenix's friends saw her as we walked up the steps and approached her. All I heard was, "Oh my gosh! Phoenix, you look amazing!"

Phoenix responded, "Well, thanks, Shannon. You look great as well!"

Shelby, Lexi and five other girls continued to compliment her. I didn't know Phoenix's friends that well as I'd only spent a brief amount of time with Shannon at the party, and I didn't really speak to Shelby and Lexi, but they definitely looked like they had fiery personalities: just sheer confidence, and maybe a bit of cockiness—just like Phoenix. The girls looked over and saw me standing next to Phoenix.

"AJ, nice to see you again," said Shannon.

"Hey, Shannon," I responded. I then looked at Shelby and said, "Shelby, I'm sorry for my brother's actions last night. That's not normally how he acts. I know you two connected last night, and I know you wanted him to be your date for today."

"Oh, no, it's okay, AJ! I appreciated the way Kevin stood up for me. I actually thought it was kinda hot," said Shelby.

I chuckled awkwardly, and we entered the high school.

Inside, the school was incredibly large for one that only hosts 500 kids. We went down a few hallways and heard a loud commotion. There was the gymnasium, but it wasn't any normal gymnasium; it was like a Chapel Hill UNC vs. Duke kind of gymnasium. It was a humongous arena, and what they did to it for the prom was even more amazing. There were lights, photo booths, fancy food buffets, and a dance floor that was out of this world. It looked like a posh club environment, and it was pretty cool.

Everyone was assigned tables at the prom, and it wasn't a coincidence that Phoenix's friends were at ours. Of course, I already knew Shelby's situation, but I wondered why six good-looking girls couldn't find a date to the prom; I guess that wasn't that important to them, and they just wanted to have fun.

The night went on, and it was very eventful. It actually allowed Phoenix and me to build a stronger bond. We danced together, took pictures, and even fed each other food in a romantic way. It felt very natural, like the two of us forgot that Phoenix had respectfully friend-zoned me months ago, but things change, I guess, and I wasn't complaining. The night was coming to an end, and it was time for the final song. Phoenix and I locked hands as we walked to the floor and prepared for a slow dance. The song began to play, and one of my hands was on Phoenix's waist, the other was holding her hand, and she was resting her head on my shoulder. It was a very intimate moment.

"You know, AJ, I had a lot of fun tonight," said Phoenix.
"Me too," I said.

Phoenix continued, "I meant to tell you this earlier, but this is one of the best times of my life and I have to thank you for it." I said thank you, but as I was going to finish my sentence, she cut me off. "I also wanted to tell you that I've been holding back a bit," she said.

Confused, I asked, "What do you mean?"

"Throughout the time we've spent together as friends, I've realized that I've been really happy," said Phoenix.

I got all giddy inside because I had a feeling of what she was going to say next, but me being me, I had to ask, "So, you're saying…?"

Phoenix went on, "I've been reluctant to do this because I've been hurt in the past, but…." She stopped talking and lifted her head off of my shoulder. Her eyes locked with mine, and then she grabbed my face. I closed my eyes as we locked lips, and it was the most sensational five seconds of my life. Granted, I'd never kissed anyone before, but the song, the setting, and the perfect girl made it feel right. I opened my eyes, and as our faces separated, I saw that she was smiling. She leaned her head on my shoulder again, and we resumed slow dancing until I started tiptoeing. I hadn't used the bathroom the entire time we were at the prom, and my bladder was about to explode!

I whispered to Phoenix, "I have to use the bathroom; I'll be right back." She said okay, and I went on my way.

I bum-rushed through the bathroom door and quickly hopped in a stall to take a piss. After two relieving minutes, I went to wash my hands. I put soap on my palms, lathered them up, and turned on the water. While washing my hands, I looked in the mirror and said to myself, "AJ, you're the man, dawg," and then I smiled.

I looked down and went to turn off the faucet. Suddenly, the lights in the bathroom turned off, and a red luminescence filled the room. I looked back up in the mirror, and my life flashed before my eyes. A black hole materialized in the mirror, and two wild demons jumped out, tackled me and pinned me to the ground. Struggling to get up and panicking at the same time, I attempted to kick my way out of their grasp. I kneed one of them, but the other one had a strong grip on me. The first one got up and grabbed me, and they both pulled me up to my feet with tight grips.

In disbelief and utter shock, I saw Insecurity standing right in front of me with red eyes stabbing through my soul and an evil smile that made me want to cringe.

"Well, I know this wasn't your ideal place for our introduction, but I got a little impatient."

"Insecurity, whatever you're thinking of doing, it's not gonna fucking happen!" I shouted.

She looked at me and said, "Aw, are you upset that I ruined your little dance with your girlfriend? Well, too fucking bad, moron; I'm trying to take over the galaxy and you, your girlfriend, your family, and all those Elisian varmints stand in my way!"

I tried to flick my shoe at her, but she dodged and it broke the mirror. Nobody outside of the bathroom could really hear the commotion since the music was so loud, and I figured I was solo dolo to take on these three. But God answered my prayer as someone knocked on the door. Phoenix was screaming on the other side!

"AJ, all you alright in there? You've been gone for quite a while now!" she said.

I tried to scream back and let Phoenix know I was in trouble, but the two stooges strapped their hands around my mouth, so everything I tried to say was muffled. Sensing something was wrong, Phoenix managed to pick the bathroom lock with her heel. With one shoe on, she saw Insecurity there with her demons holding me back, and instantly, the door closed shut and locked behind her.

"Well, if it isn't my strong and independent niece," said Insecurity.

Phoenix responded, "You're dead to me."

"That's not a nice thing to say to your auntie," responded Insecurity.

"You're not my family, so fuck off!" said Phoenix.

"I didn't need the attitude, but forget it. Sorry, not sorry; I'm ruining your prom tonight! And don't worry, I'll be back for you two," Insecurity said to us.

She snapped her fingers, and the two demons dropped me like an egg and took off. Everything in that moment was in slow motion as I watched the demons run past Phoenix and blast through the door. Phoenix went to rush Insecurity, but before she could get her hands on her, Insecurity disappeared back through the mirror. Everything that I had just seen put me in complete distress, and I started to fade off until all I saw was black. I started to regain consciousness, and Phoenix was over me, slapping my face.

"AJ, wake up! AJ, please wake up; I can't have you fade off on me now!" she said.

Blinking a few times to full consciousness, I got up.

"Oh, thank goodness. Here, take this. Those demons are going mad out there, and we've got to stop them," said Phoenix.

She handed me my laser gun as it must've fallen out of my pants when I went unconscious. Without hesitation, the two of us ran back out to the prom and saw a complete disaster. All of the decor was shredded to pieces, and the DJ booth was trashed. Everyone was running around like gazelles as the two lions chased their food. We split up as Phoenix went after one of the demons, and I went after the other. I approached the one nearest as it had its eyes set on someone. Shannon was standing straight up, shaking in place, which put a huge target on her. The demon picked up speed and lunged at her. Before he could latch on and eat her face, I shot him with no hesitation. My hand was shaking. I'd trained for a while in combat training, but actually witnessing myself put a hole in another organism—whether it was human or not—was unimaginable. As Shannon stood there, having caught the brute end of demon guts, I grabbed her arm and rushed for the exit.

Phoenix tapped my shoulder as we ran out. I guess she took the other demon out pretty quick.

In complete shock and disbelief, Shannon yelled, "Who are you guys?"

"There's no time for that right now, Shannon. Right now, you gotta come with us. Call your mom and dad and tell them you'll be safe with us," said Phoenix.

"Okay, okay. I'll call them right now," said Shannon.

We exited the high school, and outside was total chaos. The clouds were pitch black, cars were backed up, and people were roaming the streets, crazed. I looked up and my jaw dropped! A big spaceship hovered in the sky, and I knew for certain the Iniquitans had landed. The Bay Area was about to be a war zone.

I said, "How are we going to get back to the house, Phoenix? The limo's not here, and we don't have a car."

"Don't worry about that. I got us; just follow me," she said.

Shannon got off the phone with her parents and we were off! We ran all the way up the sidewalk to the peak of the traffic. Phoenix picked a car, broke the window and unlocked it.

We hopped in, but the keys weren't there.

"What are we gonna do without the keys? We can't get out of here without them," said Shannon.

Phoenix looked at me in the passenger seat and then looked at Shannon in the back seat and popped wires from the car.

"Where did you learn how to hotwire a fucking car?" asked Shannon.

"Shannon, we're in a motherfucking crisis right now; there's no need for the questions," responded Phoenix.

She put the two wires together, they sparked, and the car started. Phoenix put the car in drive, pulled the e-brake down and took off! We drove toward the estate at high speed, swerving through traffic recklessly and hitting multiple cars on the way. Sir Concord called Phoenix's phone, and I quickly picked it up since she was driving.

"Phoenix, where are you two? Are you okay?" asked Sir Concord.

I answered, "Sir Concord, it's me, AJ. Phoenix and I are okay. I'm pretty sure you know this already, but Insecurity came early, and it's not looking good."

Phoenix grabbed the phone with one hand while the other was on the steering wheel. "Dad, we're around the corner. Don't ask how, but we'll be home in ten minutes. We had to bring Shannon with us since she had nowhere to go. She called her parents, and they know she's with us."

"Okay, she'll stay with the nanny. Just get home ASAP!" said Sir Concord.

"Mr. Maxwell, what's going on? I'm scared," said Shannon.

"Shannon, just calm down. You'll be fine! Dad, I'll see you in a bit," said Phoenix.

Phoenix hung up the phone and kept driving. A couple minutes and a few crazy street runners later, we got to the house. Phoenix parked the car, and the three of us ran in while Sir Concord and Madam Serenity held the door open.

As I entered the house, my mother and father immediately grabbed me.

"Junior, are you okay?" asked my mom.

I responded with a yes.

"Thank God you're okay," said my dad.

Kevin rushed me, hyperventilating, and tried to tell me what he saw. "AJ, we was on the fuckin bridge, son, on the way back, and some spaceship shit dropped a bomb on the middle of the bridge, and the shit split in half, dawg! We were already at the end, but we could've died, AJ!"

I wanted to reassure Kevin, but I was unsure of how the situation was going to turn out. "Kevin, I need you to calm down for a second. We're gonna figure this out and end this thing," I said.

"AJ, promise me you're gonna take care of that demon lady, cuz I'm not ready to die! You see Lil Man crying? He's too young, AJ! You see Mom and Dad? They still have their whole lives ahead of them. Just please promise me you'll make this right," said Kevin.

I looked over at my family, and they were totally distraught. It was painful to see them tear up. I couldn't imagine my life without them. My family was all I had. I would sacrifice my life every chance I got just so my family could live their longest lives, and that's what I had to do.

I went to Sir Concord and said, "Sir Concord, we have to go now. We can't waste any time; the city is in complete turmoil!"

"You're right, AJ. Honey, stay back with the Hendrixes and everyone else. Stock each of the rooms with food and water, and lock all of the doors. AJ, Phoenix and I will travel back to Elise to release the troops," said Sir Concord.

Kevin blurted out, "I'm coming, too. Two Hendrixes are better than one."

"Kevin, it's alright. Just stay back with everyone else," I said.

"No, AJ, I'm not letting you go without me. For sixteen years, we've been attached. As brothers, we ride together, and we die together," said Kevin.

We hugged, and then my parents and Lil Man gave us a tight group hug.

"You two be safe, and we'll be praying for you," said my mother.

With tears streaming down his face, my dad said, "I love you both very much, and by far, you two are the most courageous young men to ever step foot on any planet.

Now, go kick Insecurity's ass and make your mom and pops proud!"

We smiled and went on our way as they waved goodbye. We went down to the basement and traveled through the portal back to Elise. As we shot out of the portal like out of a towel gun, the four of us landed back in the palace with Lucious waiting in front of us, looking all frantic.

"Your Majesty, to be truthful, we were not prepared for this!" he said.

"Lucious, I know, and as a leader of this planet, it was my fault. I should've seen this coming," said Sir Concord.

"Well, the situation is even worse. Insecurity hasn't stopped. We received word from our Earth intel that she's expanded across the entire planet in the matter of an hour, and people are dying!"

"Well, enough of the chit-chat and pity talk, Dad. Let's go! Are the troops ready, Lucious?" asked Phoenix.

Lucious responded, "Yes, everyone is ready and equipped to go!"

"Good, because we have an entire world to save!" said Phoenix.

We left the basement in the palace and headed for the yard where every single Elisian was there ready to take off to Earth.

"AJ and Kevin, you two go with Phoenix in one of the ships, and Phoenix, you drive it. Lucious and I will go on our ship."

We nodded our heads and headed to the ship. As we got ready to take off, I knew good and well that this might be my last day alive.

Phoenix hopped in the driver's seat as I went to the passenger seat and Kevin went into the back. Kevin and I grasped our hands together and bowed our heads, hoping to talk to God before the first and last battle mission of our lives.

Kevin went on to start the prayer. "Lord, God, we pray to you today before we land back on Earth to ask for your guidance and your protection as we take on the opposition and the oppressor named Insecurity. I pray you give us the strength to come out on top and bring restoration back to Earth as it should be. In your son Jesus' name, I pray," and we collectively said, "Amen!"

"AJ, we ride together, we die together," said Kevin.

Repeating him, I said, "We ride together, we die together," and we hugged it out again.

Phoenix pulled the lever as all of the other ships took off, and we followed.

CHAPTER 7
THE HEAD OF THE BEAST

Phoenix began driving at high speed through the galaxy, and Kevin and I held onto our seatbelts for dear life. We were going so fast that my lips were folding over like I was at the dentist.

"Do you even know where you're going?" asked Kevin.

Phoenix responded, "I don't know where I'm going, but this thing does," and she pointed at the front dashboard, which resembled a GPS tracker.

I asked what it was, and she told me just that and more.

"It's a GPS tracker. It's an overview of all areas on Earth, but it also tracks high volatile activity like war."

"Is that what those red dots are?" asked Kevin.

Phoenix said yes, and we saw that they were everywhere: Europe, Asia, Africa, North America, and South America. We looked closely and saw a lot of activity in the northeast region of the States.

I told Phoenix, "Zoom in on the GPS a little bit. Kev, you see where those dots are?" I asked.

A lot of them were in the lower part of New York, and we instantly knew what was up. He looked, and simultaneously we said, "The crib!"

"That bitch is definitely there, and we're gonna end her right now," said Phoenix.

My question was, what was she doing in Westchester? My family was back in the Bay; if she wasn't coming after my family, what did she want?

As we dodged through a bunch of space rocks, we descended onto Earth and headed towards the U.S. The GPS took us over the Atlantic coast. We passed by Florida, Georgia, the Carolinas, Virginia, and all the other states until we reached New York City. As we hovered in the sky, Phoenix and I looked out the window and saw the entire city destroyed. All of the buildings were torn down, people were scattering everywhere, and the only thing still intact was the Statue of Liberty.

"Ayo, Phoenix, we need to keep moving! We don't got time to waste!" yelled Kevin.

She continued to fly the ship until we reached our destination. Once we got there, we saw that the damage to Westchester resembled the same damage to New York City but was even more extensive. All the roads were split, the local grocery store near my house was demolished, and the worst part was the bodies on the ground. Regardless of whether my family felt connected to the community or not, this area was a place we called home for years, and it was sad to see the people and environment taken away. And for what? Greed? Power? Whatever Insecurity felt prosperity was? Whatever she thought this did for her wasn't with it, and she had to go.

We landed near the cul-de-sac where my home was and saw Insecurity walking through the rubble of the demolished homes, concrete, vehicles and bodies of my neighbors. We got off the ship with our guns out and drawn.

With my temper boiling, I screamed, "What the fuck do you want, Insecurity?! Why are you fucking doing this? You're over here killing people and ruining lives for fucking what?"

She stood there and laughed at my pain. "I had all of you fooled with the virus. See, that was just a distraction. I was here the whole time, and you didn't even know it. You think I was gonna wait forever to take what's mine?" she said.

She continued, "You Elisians set up shop on that small planet with your goody-two-shoes efforts to 'bring change, and make everyone equal;' well enough of that bubblegum shit. It doesn't fucking work. Some people control the power while others bow down, and that's how it should be. It is what it is, and my father set out to accomplish that. He was so close, but you Elisians took him away from me. So, now I have to finish what he started. If that means taking out anyone in the way, well, so be it."

The whole time she spoke, I stared into her eyes. I saw the red eyes that I'd seen before, but I was also able to see past them and into her soul. It was dark and empty without a sight of light. Suddenly, a small light appeared, under which a little girl cried. I couldn't grasp what I was seeing at first, but then something clicked. The little girl was Insecurity, and she was in pain. Pain, pain, pain, pain. That's all I sensed coming from Insecurity's soul, and before I left, I saw one last tear shed from the girl's face. I came back to my physical state, and that same tear I saw from the little girl came down Insecurity's face.

With an angry look on her face, Insecurity said, "Well, enough of the chatter. Soldiers!"

All of her Iniquitans appeared in the surrounding areas out of nowhere and circled around us.

"AJ, what are we gonna do, gang? We're outnumbered!" said Kevin.

Phoenix then looked at Kevin and me and winked. Kevin understood what she was signaling and said out loud, "Just say the word!"

Phoenix said, "Word," and we let off. Shooting and dodging left and right, we dropped the soldiers like flies, but there were too many of them to overcome. We got trapped, and they grabbed the three of us.

They kicked us to our knees and placed us in front of Insecurity. She grabbed me by the shirt and lifted me up. She lifted her fist and punched me in the face. I was dragged onto the ship in a disoriented state by Insecurity as her soldiers followed. Before I went unconscious, I looked back and saw Phoenix and Kevin lying face down on the ground, unmoving, with some of the soldiers standing over them. Before it all went black, my mind went straight to the gutter. I didn't want to believe that she had just taken my flesh and blood and the only girl I'd ever fallen for in my life away from me. With a countdown of ten in my head, I looked up at Insecurity and said, "Fuck you!" and then went unconscious.

It was dark for a minute, but then a light appeared. Suddenly, more light appeared, and I felt like I was laying on clouds. My eyes fully opened, and I realized I was back in the same bed as in the dream I had a while back. I hopped up out of the bed with my white robe on and ran down the spiral steps to enjoy the view of the red-sanded beach. As I reached the bottom of the steps, I saw Kevin standing at the door.

I screamed, "Kevin, you're alright!"

"Of course I'm okay. Why wouldn't I be?" asked Kevin.

I responded, "Well, I saw you…" then I paused. I didn't want to think about what I saw because Kevin was in front of me, and that was all that mattered. "Hey Kev, do you know what's going on right now?" I asked.

"Nah, do you?" he said.

"Nah, I don't. Well, there's a beach out front. Do you wanna check it out?" I asked.

"Fa sho, dawg; let's go!" said Kevin.

We exited the front door and ran out to the beach at full speed with smiles on our faces. As we got closer and closer, we could see a woman in the distance wearing a long, white silk dress. We reached the edge of the water and stopped. The woman turned around and just stood there, waiting.

Suddenly, I lost control of my legs, and they began to move automatically towards the woman in the dress. I looked back at Kevin to see if he would do something, but he just stood there like a robot. A few steps later, I was in front of the woman. To my surprise, it was Phoenix.

"Phoenix, you don't know how good it is to see you!"

Before I could say something else, she put her finger on my lips, pressed down to make my face meet hers, and kissed me. For the next ten seconds, I felt nothing but bliss until it was over. I opened my eyes, and Phoenix stood there, laughing in my face in a very creepy way. I was very confused and looked back at Kevin; what I saw left me dead inside. Blood was seeping through Kevin's face, and I saw tears streaming down his face.

I screamed, "Kevin! Kevin! Noooooo!"

I ran towards him as his body started to disintegrate, and with tears coming down, he waved bye to me.

Before I could get there in time, he was gone, and in pure pain and disbelief, I dropped to my knees and cried. While in distress, I heard the laugh get closer and closer and closer. I looked up, and Phoenix laughed with blood dripping down her face.

I looked at her in frustration and said, "What the fuck is wrong with you? You're sitting there laughing while my brother is gone? Are you crazy?"

All of a sudden, she stopped laughing. Her body froze and disintegrated just like Kevin's, but my worst nightmare appeared in front of me. The beach disappeared, and the house was gone. I started sweating as it became really hot, and there she was.

Insecurity, within two centimeters of my eyes, whispered, "Wake up!"

I woke up with my arms, legs, and the rest of my body feeling tight. Gaining full consciousness, I saw I was on the floor in shackles with two Iniquitans by my side and

Insecurity on her throne. I realized that my body was in the depths of an abyss, and I knew I was on Planet Iniquitous.

"Aw, the baby has awakened from his nap. How did you sleep?" asked Insecurity.

With pure anger and aggression, I yelled, "Shut the fuck up, and get me out of these chains so I can end you right now! I don't give a fuck about nothing anymore! You took part of my life away from me; now you gotta die!"

She laughed in the same evil way that Phoenix had in my unconscious state and signaled to her stooges. Both of them lifted me up, then simultaneously popped me in the face, and my nose began leaking.

"Now, now, Chosen One. You should know better than to disrespect your host as you're a guest in my home. But, regardless of that fact, I see potential in you.

"What are you talking about?" I asked.

She snapped her fingers again, and the stooges cut off the chains from my legs but kept the ones locked on my arms. They grabbed me and brought me to Insecurity as she went on to tell me, "I'm going to show you around Iniquitous. It'll take your mind off of Earth and that piece of shit planet you call Elise."

"Don't fucking bother. You might as well kill me now." Before I could say something else, I got punched in the mouth again.

"From now on, you only speak when spoken to," said Insecurity.

We headed out the front door of her estate and went on our way. The heat was very consistent, and the skies were red and overbearing. Iniquitous gave me the impression of what people perceived Hell to be like: hot, lackluster, droopy, and very physically and emotionally draining. I wouldn't be surprised if this was Hell and she was the devil. We kept walking, and I had to blink about twenty times to believe what I was seeing. It was like a worldwide assembly line of demons making a substance that looked like candy and putting it in bottles.

"You know what that is, don't you?" asked Insecurity.

"You made this?" I responded.

"Yes, I made this. Why are you so pressed?" Insecurity said in a joking matter.

"Fuck you!" I screamed.

"AJ, I get it. I know being a teenager is hard. I know it was difficult for you to fit in, not have your brother with you 24/7, and deal with people judging you and taking advantage of your size. I know you had trouble making friends, and people outside of your family didn't understand you."

"How do you know so much?" I asked.

"Well, you portray your problems out loud when you're in distress, and you poured your heart out when you were unconscious. I get it. Let me ask you this: How did you feel when you took your first piece of candy? Like you were in your own world? Like all of your prior problems just went away and never came back? You felt good, didn't you, AJ?" asked Insecurity.

"I will say this one more time: Fuck you! You're heartless! This candy bullshit kills people, and I would know because it almost killed me!" I screamed.

Insecurity started laughing and said, "My goodness! It seems that I struck a nerve of yours, so let me change topics."

She continued, "AJ, the thing that you and I have in common is that we both cherish the ones we love a lot."

"Yes, Insecurity. I love my family to death, so what are you getting at?" I responded.

"I want to offer you a proposition. Of course, as you know, my father was taken away from me and I had to raise myself at a young age. My mother wasn't there for me, so my dad was all I had, but he's gone. Now, imagine if you didn't have your mom and dad and brothers."

"Why should I feel pity for you when you killed my brother?!" I screamed. She smiled at me, and I didn't know why because I was serious.

"I didn't kill your brother, AJ. He's fine. I left him there unconscious with your little girlfriend because I know how much they mean to you, but I wanted you to know how it feels when they're forcefully taken away from you. Anyway, my proposition to you is that you help me take over the universe, and I'll spare your family. But if you don't, then I'll really kill your brother and the rest of your family right in front of you," said Insecurity.

I was still frustrated but relieved at the same time. My brother was still alive, which was great, but the fact that Insecurity had me believe he was gone and threatened to kill my family had my blood boiling.

I knew she was bluffing with her proposition because she would probably kill me anyway, so I looked her in the eyes and said, "You must be stupid to think I'd help you, and to be honest, I know you're hurting inside. I know you loved your father dearly, and you want to avenge him, but at what cost, Insecurity? Whatever you do is not gonna bring him back."

The tears I saw from the little girl appeared on her face, and she began to cry. She then got frustrated and smacked me across the face. She signaled to the two demons beside me.

"Take him back to the estate now, and lock him in the basement."

They grabbed my arms and started dragging me away. Ten minutes later, we finally got back. One of the demons opened the front door as the other pushed me through it. They brought me down a flight of stairs to a room with a huge lock on the door. One of them pulled a key from their pocket, unlocked the door, threw me inside and closed the door behind me.

I was locked in a dungeon with very dim lighting. I managed to roll over, and all I saw were the skeletal remains of dead bodies! By the obvious looks of it, Insecurity liked to keep the remains of her victims as souvenirs, and I was scared that I'd end up like that next.

I screamed, "Let me out of here!" but of course, that wasn't going to do me any good. All I could hope for at this point was a miracle—a miracle that was going to bring me out of here alive and back to my family. So, I closed my eyes, hoping that I'd be out of this dungeon when I woke up and everything would be back to normal.

CHAPTER 8
THE END IS NEAR

I woke up to several loud noises, and it made my heart race. I didn't know what was going on out there, so I started squirming around and panicking. Then, suddenly, I heard a voice screaming, "AJ! AJ, are you in there, gang?"

I instantly knew it was Kevin, so I screamed back, "Kevin, I'm down here!"

"Okay, gang! We coming down right now!" he said.

I was happy that they were here to rescue me, but how were they going to open the door? Out of nowhere, the door exploded, and Kevin and Lucious were there. The two of them saw me on the floor, and Kevin said, "Shit, he's in shackles. How are we getting them shits off of him?"

Lucious looked towards Kevin's side and took his laser gun. He pointed it and shot at the chain links on my shackles, and I was able to break free. They both picked me up off the ground, and Lucious said, "AJ, we have to get you out of here, now! It's madness out there!"

We exited the dungeon and left the estate. As we emerged outside, the scene was absolutely insane. The candy factory was destroyed, homes were demolished and Iniquitous was a complete battlefield. Elisian drones flew at high speeds, shooting lasers, and soldiers jumped out of them with parachutes. The people of Iniquitous were firing back with their own artillery, and all of the chaos was leaving a bunch of bodies behind. The three of us ran to the battle to help our people and put an end to the war. We started dodging bombs and lasers and hid behind one of the houses for shelter. From a distance, I could see Phoenix whooping ass. She kicked, chopped and punched Iniquitans left and right, with no problem, and didn't even have to shoot her laser gun once. I then saw my parents in the line of battle, and I was shocked. My mother was badass, and my dad was doing a bunch of flips and tricks that I'd never seen before. My parents never trained for battle, so how were they so elusive and coordinated?

I stepped out from my hiding space as I felt that I should be the one to defeat Insecurity. Kevin looked at me and said, "AJ, what are you doing? You can't go out there without a heater."

Lucious looked at me and said, "Catch," as he threw me his laser gun.

I caught it and thanked him, then ran back into the battle to put my training to use—as well as take Insecurity's head off. I started dropping one Iniquitan after another with the laser gun, and I was finally able to get Insecurity in my sights. She was on top of Sir Concord and beating him up, bad. Madam Serenity was on the ground, badly injured, and I could only assume that was the work of Insecurity. With my body filled with rage, I ran as fast as I could, like a cheetah hunting its prey, and once I was within reach, I lunged at Insecurity and tackled her to the ground.

I picked her up, put the laser gun to her head and said, "Tell me why I shouldn't just kill you right now?"

She started to laugh and said, "Well, why don't you just do it then?"

She didn't have to tell me twice; once she said that, I was ready to pull the trigger, but I suddenly heard Phoenix scream, "AJ, stop!"

I looked around and everyone, including the Iniquitans, just stopped. All the guns and other weapons dropped to the ground, the flying drones landed, and all eyes were on me.

"AJ, don't do it, please. Killing her isn't going to bring justice to all the people she killed and all the families she ruined," said Phoenix.

She was right. Killing Insecurity was her easy way out, and she wouldn't be able to take responsibility for what she did. So, I looked at Phoenix, dropped my gun and handed Insecurity to two Elisian soldiers who cuffed her hands behind her back.

Sir Concord then ordered them to take Insecurity onto his drone wait there with her until he was ready to board. He picked up Madam Serenity from the ground and then turned to me and said, "AJ, thank you."

"Sir Concord, where are you going to take her?" I asked.

Madam Serenity butted in and said, "To prison! We've been in talks with the President of the United States, and there's an isolated cell waiting for her at Rikers Island."

I guess prison was the best alternative. Insecurity would have plenty of time to drive herself insane in isolation and truly think about what she did and the lives she affected.

"Everyone get in your drones and head back to Elise. Phoenix, take AJ and his family with you on your drone and follow us," said Madam Serenity.

"But what about all these Iniquitans?" asked Phoenix.

"What about them? They caused the damage as well, and since we can't take them all on the drones, our only choice is to leave them here with nothing," said Sir Concord.

All of us Elisians looked back and saw the looks on the Iniquitans' faces. They were pleading, and we looked at each other, knowing they contributed to the madness but also that it wasn't their choice. But, we turned away, loaded up on the drones and left Iniquitous as the war was over.

Phoenix got in the driver's seat and I sat in the passenger seat. My parents and Kevin sat in the back, and while we were riding through space, I had a few questions to ask my parents.

"Mom, Dad, where's Lil Man?" I asked.

"Oh, he's with the babysitter back in San Fran," said my mom.

"Phoenix pinged her father her location after you were taken by Insecurity, so when he relayed that to us, we traveled through the portal back to Elise so we could help save you," said my dad.

I asked, "Dad, where did you learn all those crazy flips and moves? You didn't train with Kev and me."

"Well, you know I like my martial arts movies, and the *Ip Man* series really paid off," said my dad.

"You know, we are really proud of you boys! We don't know any other teenage boys who could do anything you two have done!" said my mom.

She continued, "Especially you, Junior. Being the chosen one in a new world and having the responsibility to protect it is unthinkable, but you managed to do it. You also showed maturity. You could've ended things with Insecurity way differently, but you didn't, and I'm proud of you,"

I looked back at her and smiled as we continued to follow Madam Serenity and Sir Concord back to Earth.

CHAPTER 9
CHANGE OF PLANS

As we cruised through the galaxy on our way back to Earth, Phoenix received a ring on the dashboard, and it was Madam Serenity calling.

"Phoenix, there's been a slight change of plans," she said.

"What do you mean?" asked Phoenix.

"Unfortunately, we have more problems to deal with. Insecurity has revealed that some world government officials helped her infiltrate the killer virus and the candy into Earth. So, we not only have to bring them to justice, but we have to inform the public as they have the right to know. Meet us at the White House, and tell AJ's parents that his younger brother is doing alright. He's still with Shannon and the sitter, and they're safe."

My parents jumped in and simultaneously said, "We need to go back to our baby boy!"

"Of course. Phoenix, you drop them back at the estate and bring AJ and Kevin with you to meet us at the White House," said Madam Serenity

Phoenix responded, "I gotchu, Mom," and went back to the Bay.

As we descended to Earth at high speed, we looked out the drone windows to see the beautiful clouds and blue sky, but it was a fairly quick view. As we swerved left and right, I could finally see the city structure and the demolished

Golden Gate Bridge, and I knew we had reached San Francisco. Kevin looked out the window and down onto the city and realized many people were staring up at the drone, thinking aliens had come back to Earth.

"Phoenix, you're drawing a lot of attention, dawg. I think you're flying too low," said Kevin.

My parents and I nodded in agreement with Kevin. Phoenix—not noticing how low she was flying—said, "Oh, snap! Let me pull up the drone right now!"

Phoenix elevated the drone and went higher into the sky so we wouldn't be seen. She followed the red dot on the dashboard which marked her Hillsborough estate. She landed in the backyard safely and dropped my parents off. They waved goodbye as we left for the White House.

I put the new destination on the dashboard GPS. Phoenix lifted off, and we were out like a light. The ride was only fifteen minutes, but Kevin chopped it up a bit with me before we arrived.

"You know, AJ, if you think of it, we're like younger, more futuristic *Bad Boys*," said Kevin.

"So, I'm Will Smith and you're Martin Lawrence?" I asked.

"Hell yeah! I'm the cooler, more funnier one, obviously! You all serious and shit," said Kevin.

I laughed hard and said to Kevin, "You know what? You're right. When this is all said and done, are you gonna tell Shelby about this?"

"Well, duh. Shawty gotta know I helped save the world, and she's gonna see too. When that news camera turns on us, we're gonna be global, baby!" said Kevin.

I started chuckling again and laughed so hard that I fell out of my seat and accidentally knocked Phoenix onto the floor. With Kevin and I reacting to our comedic moment, neither of us realized we were descending at an even faster speed than normal. The drone then started making loud, alarming beeping noises, and they caught our attention.

Phoenix angrily said, "AJ, what the fuck?"

"Phoenix, I'm so sorry," I responded.

The drone system began to speak: "Vehicle destructing in 20 seconds. Descending at high speeds. Ascend immediately."

"I got this, I got this," I said. I got up and grabbed the wheel.

Kevin began to panic. "AJ, you better pull this bitch up right now! We can't die right now!"

I pulled on the steering wheel in an upward motion as hard as I could and screamed, "I'm trying, Kev. We're not gonna die! We're not gonna die!"

As we descended, we could see the White House; we were going to crash into it head-on if I didn't do something. It wasn't looking good, so Kev grabbed onto my shoulder.

In distress, he said, "Well, if I'm gonna die, at least I'm dying with my brother," and then he closed his eyes.

"We better not die!" screamed Phoenix.

As we became closer to the White House, the drone wasn't rising, so I decided to swerve the wheel to the right while screaming to see if that would do anything. Surprisingly, it worked, but it didn't leave us without any damage. We ended up crashing on the front lawn of the White House. The front window shattered, the back of the drone busted wide open, the dashboard got jacked up, and the three of us were in a complete daze.

My head was pounding, and I could see lines of red dripping down my legs. I definitely had some scrapes and bruises, and I was hoping I hadn't broken anything. I looked over at Kevin, and he was in the same shape as me. Surprisingly, Phoenix came out with just a few minor bumps and managed to stay on her feet. I crawled over to Kevin to make sure he was okay. He nodded to me, affirming he was, and then Phoenix helped the two of us get back on our feet. We hobbled out of the drone, and I saw Madam Serenity running full steam ahead at us.

"Oh my goodness, are you two okay? What happened?" she asked.

"These dickheads were fooling around, and AJ knocked me off the wheel!" said Phoenix.

Phoenix looked at me, and I responded, "It was my fault. I take responsibility."

"Ugh, Mom, forget it; there's no time. We have to get inside the White House," said Phoenix.

In the distance, I could see Concord walking up the steps with Insecurity, who was in cuffs, but guns were drawn at them by the White House security at the entrance. Madam Serenity grabbed all of us and dragged us toward Sir Concord and Insecurity. As we caught up with them, the secret service agents drew their rifles in our faces.

One agent blurted out, "Don't take one more step, or we'll shoot."

"We want no issues here. We have arrived to speak to the higher power as it is very important news," said Concord.

"Where's the president?" asked Madam Serenity.

All of a sudden, the president walked out with the vice president and put his hand down on one of the agent's guns. That was a signal for the agents to relax and stand back.

"Concord, Serenity, is everything okay?" asked the president.

"Almost everything, to be honest, Mr. President. We have Insecurity here in our custody, and the carnage is over. But, she has revealed to us that some important individuals on Earth helped infiltrate the killer virus and her candy substance that has taken the lives of many around the world, and one of those people resides in this building," said Concord.

"Well, I don't believe that anyone within my camp would demonstrate such a demonic and monstrous act, but Concord and Serenity, I've known you two for years, and I trust your word. Who is it?" asked the president.

I looked closely and could see the vice president's hands start to shake. I could tell by his movements that he was guilty. Before Concord could spill the beans, the vice president reacted. He lunged at one of the secret service agent's rifles to try and disperse a hundred rounds of bullets amongst us all, but the agent put up a fight. Concord then lunged at the vice president and brought him down to the ground.

"Mr. Vice President, your time is up," said Concord.

"Ah, fuck you," said the vice president.

"How could this be; why on Earth would he do this?!" screamed the president.

Concord brought the vice president to his feet as he began to say, "The whole plan was for Insecurity to obtain world domination, and the two of us would share power. Not only would I be the ruler of the world, but I'd take your spot as the president."

The president was disgusted with his former running mate and ordered him to be taken away along with Insecurity. Serenity let go of Insecurity and let the U.S. government agents take hold of her. Phoenix asked the president where they would be taking the vice president.

"He'll join Insecurity at Rikers Island," said the president. He continued, "We have even more issues that lie ahead of us. This is a global problem; there are political leaders beyond the U.S. government who have been involved, so I have to call the UN leaders. Also, this will get out pretty fast, so the press will be everywhere! I will have to make a statement, and you all will have to as well, so be prepared!"

Hearing that made me nervous. I'd never been on camera before in my life, and being on camera for the first time during a global broadcast was a lot of pressure.The president waved us all in as we made our way to the Oval Office. He got on the phone as quickly as possible to alert other UN leaders about traitors within their government circles. He then received a call from his secretary letting him know that the press was outside.

"Are you all ready?" asked the president.

"Damn straight—I mean, yes sir, Mr. President," said Kevin.

Everyone else agreed, and we set out to meet the press in front of the White House. Surrounded by the secret service agents, we met the hundreds of reporters, cameras, and microphones in our faces as we were asked questions.

"Mr. President, can you explain to us what exactly is going on, one with the huge drone on the lawn, and two, with the status of the galaxy war?" asked one reporter.

"To answer your first question, behind me are Concord Maxwell, Serenity Maxwell, Phoenix Maxwell, Kevin Hendrix, and AJ Hendrix. They are members of Planet Elise, a universally advanced planet with individuals who have been protecting Earth from intergalactic threats and supplying our planet with the technology that we've had for many years. Elisians have been on Earth for hundreds of years and have lived amongst the normal human population. The drone is here because these five have arrived to bring Ms. Insecurity Bane to justice as she has been a universal threat to our existence for years. Because of this, the galaxy war has ended!"

All of the reporters screamed with joy, and I could only imagine what everyone around the world was feeling as well.

"There have been reports that high-ranked political officials aided Ms. Bane's plan on world domination; is this true?" asked another reporter.

Concord then butted in and said, "We have discovered that the vice president gave his services to Insecurity in order to obtain the president's current position in hopes of the president being eliminated. The vice president isn't the only government official, as you all may know now. The president has informed all of the head officials of countries of the United Nations that they have rotten tomatoes within their circles. We expect them to be reprimanded and criminally held responsible for their actions as well."

"This question is for Mr. Maxwell. What was everyone's role in taking down Insecurity and restoring world order to Earth?" asked another reporter.

"As the president mentioned, beside me is my wife, my daughter, Kevin Hendrix—who's the brother of the chosen warrior of our Planet Elise—and AJ Hendrix. These two, and especially AJ, should be receiving all of the praise as their bravery, wit, perseverance, and compassion were instrumental in bringing Insecurity to justice."

The cameras switched from Concord and the president to Kevin and me. All the flashing lights, microphones, and people in my face were very intimidating, but this was my moment.

"Question for the Hendrix boys: Being so young, what was the pressure like for you two to bring Insecurity down with the fate of Earth's humanity in your hands?"

Before I could say something, Kevin determined it was his time to shine.

"Ayo, listen up!" he said. "We had to go through some shit to take that crazy lady down. We had to go through nonstop combat training and learn to drive them dope-ass drones. My brother and I might have to touch up a bit on that, but y'all wouldn't understand."

I said, "What my brother is trying to say is that our lives within the past year have been a rollercoaster. My life prior to Elise wasn't what I wanted it to be. I never really fit in at school or in my community. I was looked over, ignored, discriminated against, and it all made me feel less of myself. The friends that I had made at a younger age branched out and associated themselves with other people. Whether my pain was caused by myself or others, I felt alone and isolated outside of my home. It is my family that keeps me here to this day. They are my backbone, my peace and happiness, and all of those factors that made me feel less of myself just went away."

I continued, "Although by prophecy, I was destined to be the chosen one, the Maxwells took me in as their own and gave me the same feeling that I had with my parents. All the doubts that I dealt with disappeared as I trained, recovered and built relationships with people from a beautiful planet. I finally felt comfortable in my own skin and who I was. When I faced Insecurity, I had the utmost confidence that she would be defeated. I also just want to say for all the families that lost loved ones because of Insecurity's actions, we did this for you."

Applause circled around the reporters, bringing smiles to people's faces. Some of the reporters asked the president if they could come up and give me a hug or thank me, and permission was granted. I stepped away from the podium to let the president continue to speak as a decent amount of reporters lined up to greet me and thank me for my words and message.

"As these brave individuals risked their lives to restore world order to our Planet Earth, it gives me nothing but great pleasure to present them with these," said the president. He reached back and grabbed medals from one of the agents.

"These here are seven Medals of Honor. They will be presented to the five brave individuals up here. As I have been told by Concord Maxwell, AJ's parents, Marcus Hendrix and Tanya Hendrix, played a significant role in helping defend us against Insecurity. Unfortunately, they could not be here today, so I will be handing AJ and Kevin these medals to give to their parents."

He went by each of us, one by one, placing the medals over our heads and then handing Kev and me our parents' medals. The press conference was then over as the reporters left, and we returned to the Oval Office.

"My dawg, we got motherfuckin' medals!" said Kevin.

"Yeah, I know. It's crazy, Kev. I honestly thought Medals of Honor were for the military," I said.

"Well, we're recognized heroes now, AJ!" said Kevin.

The president then thanked us again. "I can't thank you all enough for what you have done. You've really saved billions of lives."

"What will happen to all the infrastructure and global neighborhoods destroyed?" I asked.

"I actually got word that after your speech, many of the world's top corporations reached out wanting to donate to infrastructure rehabilitation," said the president.

"Oh my gosh, that's great!" screamed Phoenix.

"Oh, that's just grand!" said Serenity.

"Well, Mr. President, we best get on our way back to the Bay," said Concord.

"Of course, of course, and when you return back to Elise, thank the people there. To the Elisians that reside on Earth as well, I will send them a personal thanks," said the president.

"What about our drone?" asked Kevin.

Serenity then looked towards the president and said, "Would you want to fix it up and keep it? For military purposes, of course."

With an excited look on his face, the president agreed, and the Royals gave our broken drone to the U.S. government. It was getting late in D.C., so we left the White House, boarded Madam Serenity and Sir Concord's drone, and headed back to the Hillsborough mansion. As we returned to the Bay, we entered the estate with my parents, Lil Man, and the babysitter standing there.

"Where's Shannon?" asked Phoenix.

"Her parents came by to pick her up. They said thanks for keeping her safe!" said the babysitter.

My parents were all giddy and happy to see us, as they had seen the press conference on the news. "We're so proud of you both!" they said collectively.

My parents and Lil Man then gave us a hug. Kevin and I pulled out their medals and put them over their heads.

"Oh my! Medals of Honor. I can't believe it. I really can't believe it," said my father.

"Your father and I have the TV on in the common area, and they're broadcasting the members of the UN who were involved," said my mother.

"Let's go see!" said Phoenix.

We all ran to the common area where the TV was tuned into the news. The news anchor lady began to speak. "Coming live from channel seven news, Bay Area, we have word that high-ranked global officials, along with the Vice President of the United States, have been arrested and brought to justice. The French prime minister, the UK prime minister, and the Australian prime minister have all been arrested for their involvement in aiding the world terror caused by one Insecurity Bane. More details in the upcoming hours."

"Woah, this is some next-level shit. It really be your own people," said Kevin.

"Yeah, son, you're right," said my father.

"It really is such a shame; so sad," said Phoenix.

Suddenly, Kevin's phone started going off. He picked it up, and I looked over his shoulder to see what was up. All I could see were nonstop notifications popping up. His phone was lighting up so much I was surprised that it didn't catch on fire!

"I just gained 200 million followers on my socials within minutes! That's more followers than Drake, AJ!" said Kevin.

Phoenix then checked her phone that she had placed on the table. "I got 205 million! Oh my gosh, this can't be real! I have to be dreaming!" she screamed.

"Well, I'm glad you're all excited, but remember that with a lot of fame comes a lot of pressure and responsibility," said Concord.

"AJ, why don't you have a social media account? I bet the people would want to hear from you," said Phoenix.

"You know what? That would be a great idea, Phoenix; why don't you or Kevin go live and let AJ send a public message out to the people?" said Serenity.

"I'll do it," said Phoenix. She went on her social media page and went live, racking up millions of live viewers in seconds just to hear us speak.

She turned the camera to herself and began to talk. "Hello, world! As you may know by now, my name is Phoenix Maxwell, and this is Kevin Hendrix and AJ Hendrix. We are the three teens who saved the world, and we just appreciate the love and support from everyone recently."

She then turned the camera to me as I began to speak. "What's going on, everyone! AJ here. Um, I just want to say that what we did wasn't easy, but we did it for all of you guys. This world was in a downward spiral for a while, and all we wanted to do was bring it back to an upward trajectory. Insecurity has manipulated the lives of many of your families and friends, and I send my condolences to the ones who lost their loved ones. What the three of us and the rest of our Elisian people promise you all is that we will always be here to protect this planet from danger. Well, anyway, we love you all. Everything is being rebuilt so we can get back to normal, and we'll see you all soon."

Phoenix then ended the live video and suggested something to me. "Let's make your social media page, AJ!"

"Yeah, you need one, dawg!" said Kevin.

"Well, I don't know; I'm not too big on the socials ," I said.

"Well, we're making you one anyway," said Phoenix.

She grabbed my phone and from there, she made a profile for me. I instantly gained 250 million supporters, but that wasn't important. What was important to me was that the world would go back to normal, and we could all live our lives again.

Everyone in the house came in for a group hug as we reminisced what a crazy day it had been. We all got ready to retire for the night, and I changed into my pajamas and set to go to sleep as my family and I were heading back to New York the next morning. Before I laid my head to rest, Phoenix came knocking on the door.

"Hey, AJ, can we talk?" she asked.

I rubbed my eyes twice and said, "Of course, of course, come in!"

She closed the door and went to lay on the bed next to me with her face and eyes looking up towards the ceiling.

"So, you're really leaving tomorrow," said Phoenix.

"Yeah. We can't go home for obvious reasons, but we have family in Long Island that's letting us stay until everything's rebuilt. Their house didn't get that much damage, to my surprise," I said.

"Well, I don't want you to leave, Junior," said Phoenix.

As she leaned her head on my shoulder, I said, "Hey, only my mother calls me Junior."

"Why does your mom call you Junior, anyway?" asked Phoenix.

"Because I'm named after my grandpa or my 'Pop Pop.' His name is Alan Hendrix, and my name is Alan Hendrix, hence AJ or Junior," I said. "I know we'll be separated for a bit, but I'm sure I'll be back for your graduation. Besides, a bit of distance won't hurt us. You have my number; I have yours, and we can video chat every day.

"That reminds me, have you heard from any colleges yet? You know, that's a big step, Phoenix!" I said.

She took her head off my shoulder and stared into my eyes intensely. "Yes, I have, and I don't know where I'm going yet, but never mind that. May I ask you an important question?" said Phoenix. I said sure, and she asked, "What are we exactly?"

"Well, I don't know, Phoenix. I like you a lot, you like me a lot, so what do you think we are?" I said.

Unexpectedly, she started to tear up, and I was completely confused. I didn't know if I had insulted her or said something wrong. I was trying to insinuate that we were in a relationship, thinking she was on the same page, but I didn't really know.

"AJ, I know that when you first met me, I might've seemed a little standoffish, but as we got to know each other and trained together and hung out, I really started to like you a lot. I thought that your little love obsession was really cute, and even though I didn't show it, I was truly happy when you were around. I just was a little reluctant because I've liked a guy before and I got my feelings hurt, and since I caught feelings for you fast, I'm a little scared," said Phoenix.

I felt like I got shot in the heart with a bazooka and my body exploded into pieces. I'd dealt with rejection before, but this one hurt a lot; I had to stay strong. I couldn't go back to the old AJ. "So, what you're saying is we shouldn't be together?" I asked.

"No, no, no, AJ!" She grabbed the front of my shirt like the bullies do and continued, "I mean that I'm all in, and I want to make sure you are, too! I'm falling hard for you, and I would rather know now whether you feel the same way or not!"

With her grip getting tighter and tighter, I asked, "Phoenix, could you let go for a second? Your grip is like an anaconda around my neck." She let go, and as I took a deep breath, I continued, "Girl, I'd be crazy not to go the distance with you. I'm surprised that any guy at that prissy rich high school you go to would turn you down. They must be on that candy bullshit, and Insecurity had them fucked up."

We both laughed quietly as I reassured her, "I know for a fact that my head won't turn. I know we're both young, but when it comes to me, I know what I want, and I stick to the end with it. I can even spit shake on that."

I reached out my hand, but before I could do anything else, Phoenix said, "Nope, that's okay. That's all I needed to hear." She smiled and locked lips with me for a few seconds and then proceeded to hug me.

"Again, too tight!" I said. "It's getting late, and I'm pretty sure your parents wouldn't want you in here with me right now."

"I don't care, AJ. I'm staying here with you. I'll leave before they wake up in the morning," said Phoenix.

"Okay, but I'm leaving at ten in the morning, so if you get up before me, wake me up, please," I said.

"Of course, of course, babe!" she said.

We then laid our heads down, turned our backs to each other and went to bed as my time here in the estate and the Bay Area wound down. Eight in the morning arrived the next day, and Phoenix was standing over me, shaking me in a frantic matter. She was visibly panicking, and I was confused as to why.

"AJ, wake up! AJ, wake up!" said Phoenix.

I rubbed my eyes multiple times in a tired state, asking what was wrong. "What's the matter, Phoenix?"

"My father is up earlier than normal. He's in the bathroom right now, and if I try to leave this room right now, he'll definitely see me."

"Well, isn't your room down the hall?" I asked.

"Exactly, and the first thing he does every morning is go to my room to wake me up. Oh my god, oh my god! We're so dead!" said Phoenix.

We both went to the door and popped it open in the slightest to see where Sir Concord was heading. He turned from the bathroom and made a left, straight for Phoenix's room down the hall. He kept walking and walking and walking, and the two of us were shaking, anticipating the trouble coming our way. Then, all of a sudden, he turned around and held his stomach. "Woah, I guess I'm a little gassy this morning," he said. Concord then ran straight back to the bathroom and closed the door.

"Go, go, go, Phoenix," I said.

She opened the door and ran to her room before her father could get out of the bathroom.

CHAPTER 10
BACK TO LIFE, BACK TO REALITY

An hour and a half passed, and it was nearly time to leave. Before we set off, the Maxwells offered breakfast. They said that the babysitter was making pancakes, bacon, and eggs for us. That combo was my absolute favorite, but I never knew how to make it, so I asked the babysitter and the Maxwells if I could help, and they said, "Sure, AJ!"

I hopped in the kitchen with the sitter. She showed me how to make pancakes from scratch and how to make scrambled eggs. The bacon part was easy as I just had to cook it on the skillet for a few minutes. While I was cooking, I decided to ask the sitter a few questions.

"If you don't mind me asking, what is your name?"

"My name is Nicole, but you can call me Nicki."

"How long have you been with the Maxwells, Nicki?" I asked.

"Five years," she said.

"If you don't mind me asking, how old are you?"

"I'm 24, AJ. I just finished my graduate degree in information systems at USF last year," she said.

"So why are you here?" I asked.

She responded, "I actually work for them at their tech company. I was an intern there; the higher-ups saw my hard work and told Ms. Serenity and Mr. Concord of my efforts in the Informatics department, and I helped them make some big bucks! It then led me to the Maxwells, and I told them my personal story. I was an orphan for the majority of my life. I finally found foster parents who brought me in at the age of 16. They took really good care of me. They enrolled me into a nice high school, attended all of my swim meets after I joined the swim team, and were there for me when I walked across the stage and graduated high school."

"I feel like there isn't a good end to this story," I said.

"Not really, AJ. My parents passed away in a car accident a few months after my graduation, and I had nobody else to turn to. I was 18, so I was legally an adult. I had just gotten into SFU, and I was set tuition-wise for the year because my parents had set aside some cash for a year's tuition and books, but I had nowhere to stay. I had no other family to reach out to, and I didn't really have money myself, so I stayed in a shelter and worked a few part-time jobs to have enough to take care of my essentials. Then, in school, I applied for an internship at LyveWire, and I got it.

"I used every little dollar I had to get to that internship each and every day and sacrificed a few meals along the way. The Maxwells heard my story and wanted to do whatever they could to help, so they offered me a place to stay with nothing in return. Phoenix didn't understand why their parents were bringing in this new girl to her home, so they said I was the babysitter they hired to watch her when they went away, which is what I did, and I've been here ever since."

"Wow, you've had a tough life. I want you to know you're a strong individual, though, and my condolences for your loss," I said.

"Well, thank you, AJ. You have to be strong in life. The world throws a lot at us to make us feel less of ourselves, and you just have to stay true to who you are and find something that motivates you to keep going. When I was in high school, I had people make fun of my weight and me being an orphan all the time. I endured a lot of fat jokes and had people say to me, 'I'm surprised they let whales join the swim team with your fat ass,' and 'You're a reject. Your real parents didn't want you.' It makes you feel worthless and ostracized from the world, and trust me, I cried many nights. Still, my main goal was to make my foster parents proud and become the successful woman I wanted to be and they wanted me to be."

I stood there in silence because I didn't know what else to say. She was absolutely right, and honestly, I wished more people were like Nicki, Phoenix, Kevin, Phoenix's parents, and my parents. I wished people would stop being selfish, belligerent, and distasteful to others by using things such as money, physical appearance, and hurtful words to hide their insecurities and project them onto others.

Nicki looked at me and said, "Let's get off my sob story and focus on not burning these pancakes."

"Oh, of course, of course," I responded.

I had one more thing on my mind to ask Nicki, so I went ahead and said, "Do you always make the meals and clean around here?"

"My goodness, another question, AJ?" said Nicki.

"My apologies. I didn't know I was bothering you," I said.

"I was just playing, AJ, and to answer your question, no, I don't always make the meals here. I only know how to make basic things such as this breakfast here and pasta dishes like fettuccine alfredo and penne alla vodka, but even so, the Maxwells come in and either help out or make stuff of their own for all of us to enjoy. The same thing goes for cleaning around the house. I do it because I feel grateful for what this family has done for me, but they clean up around the house as well. I'm not really the sitter or the nanny around here, but Phoenix called me that when we first got introduced, so now everyone calls me that as a cute nickname."

We moved on from my question and finished cooking breakfast. We began to plate the food and place it in front of everyone at the table, and everyone's eyes lit up. They were excited to eat the delicious meal while enjoying the last meal we all might have together for at least the next couple of months.

"Nicki, AJ, this looks amazing! Thank you!" said my father.

"This meal is delicious, but we have to hurry it up. We don't want to miss our flight, guys," my mom said.

"Oh, don't worry about your flight. Take your time," said Madam Serenity.

"Ser—I mean, Madam Serenity, what are you talkin' 'bout?" asked Kevin.

"I canceled your flight as Concord and I got a private charter for you to go back to New York," she responded. Concord nodded and smiled.

"But what about my money?" asked my mom.

"Check your phone; you should've gotten your money back," said Concord.

My mom checked her phone and there the notification was. "My bad," she said.

"How did you even cancel it?" I asked.

"I called the airport and asked for the last name Hendrix. They found your tickets, and I asked them to cancel them," Serenity responded.

"Woah, I kinda feel dumb," I said.

"Stay for another hour so we can enjoy this meal and chat more. We held the charter for 11, so you have some time," said Concord.

"Sure, why not, and let me just say this, Concord and Serenity. We are very thankful and appreciative for what you have done for us, truly," said my father.

"Oh, it's alright! Besides, Marcus, Serenity and I notice people with great character when we see them, and that's what you, your wife and your boys are. You remind us of ourselves."

Madam Serenity butted in, "Plus, you are descendants of a man who holds a tremendous importance in our Elisian society, so whatever we do for you all, we feel honored in doing so."

"Well, amen to that, ya feel me?!" screamed Kevin.

He raised his glass of orange juice, and we all followed to cheers and then continued to enjoy our breakfast. Then, out of nowhere, Kevin's phone began to ring.

He answered, "Yello, you talkin' to a real one, Kevin Hendrix. Who am I speaking with? Shelby? Oh shit! Girl, what you doing calling me this early? Hold on."

He quickly got up out of his seat and ran to the bathroom. In the distance, I heard him say, "Girl, you know I'm leaving today to go back to New York and shit. Just call me when I land. Aight, peace."

"Who's he talking to, AJ? And don't lie to me," said my mom.

Phoenix intervened and said, "That's my friend, Shelby."

"How'd the two of them meet?" My mom asked.

"At Shannon's party. The three of us snuck out while you all were sleeping, but we didn't stay that long since AJ had a panic attack and Kevin almost beat a kid to death, but that's not important," said Phoenix.

All the adults at the table started laughing as they believed what Phoenix had just said was a joke. Phoenix, realizing she snitched on all of us by accident, began laughing with them to play it off.

"Anyway, speaking of a girlfriend, what are you two gonna do? We all see the bond between you two, and New York is a long way from California, you know," said my mother.

All eyes—from my parents and Phoenix's—were on us as we looked at each other.

"We're together, and we'll stay together. I know the distance is a factor, but AJ and I talked, and we're gonna get through it," said Phoenix.

"Yeah, what she said," I responded, and we hugged each other.

My parents and hers smiled simultaneously, and Madam Serenity said, "Aw, look at you two lovebirds. You look perfect together."

"And you have my full permission, AJ," said Sir Concord.

"Likewise our way, Phoenix. We're glad you make our son happy, and when he's happy, we're happy," said my father.

Kevin then came back, and the attention turned towards him.

"What y'all looking at?" he asked.

My mom gave him a stern look, and Kevin finally opened up. "Okay, Mama, I got a lil' lady friend I've been talking to, and I was gonna tell you."

"Kev, you know I care a lot about you boys, and I just don't want anyone to hurt your feelings," said my mom.

"I know, I know, Mama," said Kevin.

My mom asked him, "So when will I meet Ms. Shelby, huh?"

"Whenever we come back out here," said Kevin.

"Well, I'm happy for you, son!" said my father.

"Thanks, Dad!" said Kevin. He began to laugh and did a little dance as everyone else smiled.

We finished our meal before we headed off. Finally, with our bags at the door and the cab out front, it was time to say goodbye to the Maxwells for now.

"Well, it's been one hell of an adventure," said my father.

"It sure has, Marcus, and once again to you and your family, thank you. Don't be a stranger, and hop through that portal every now and then," responded Concord.

"Yo, C-man, you already know we in there! Shit was a movie, and it ain't even over yet," said Kevin.

I laughed hard, but my pops tapped both of us on our shoulders. "Kev, language!"

"Sorry, Pops," said Kevin.

"I know you'll be here for my grad, but for the time being, phone and portal?" asked Phoenix.

"Phone and portal, babes," I told Phoenix.

She smiled and kissed me on the cheek as we left through the door and headed into the cab. We closed the cab doors, and before we left, we all waved bye.

"Bye, guys. Thanks for having us," I said.

"Bye, Nicki! Bye, Nicki!" screamed Lil' Man.

"Bye, Cameron! Bye, Cameron!" screamed Nicki.

We took off in the cab and said goodbye to Hillsborough and the Bay Area as we headed to the airport to go back to New York. We reached the airport and got our bags checked through security. While that was going on, many people started clapping and screaming, "Thank you! Thank you all for saving us!"

Kevin began to bow. "You're welcome. You're welcome."

I picked Kevin up and said, "Get your ass up, Kev. We gotta go."

As we passed through security, our charter was there waiting for us along with the pilot.

"Nice to see the Hendrix family again. I just want to say thank you. I didn't know that the Maxwells and you all were like superhumans or alien humans or whatever y'all are. I just thought they were rich tech gurus."

"Well, we didn't find out ourselves until this year," said my mother.

"Well, what are we waiting for? Let's get going. Mrs. Hendrix, your brother, Landon, and his wife are on their way to the landing spot to pick y'all up," said the pilot.

"I haven't seen Uncle Landon in a minute, bruh," said Kevin.

"Yeah, that's facts, Kev," I said.

"Facts, Kev," Lil Man repeated.

We laughed, went on the plane, strapped up and took off.

Six hours later, we reached New York. We got off the plane, thanked the pilot and saw Uncle Landon and his wife waiting in their SUV.

"How was the flight, my superheroes?" asked my uncle.

"It was nice," said my mother.

"It was fire, Unc!" said Kevin.

"Fire, Unc!" repeated Lil' Man.

"That's good. Well, buckle up. We'll be at the house in an hour or so," said Uncle Landon.

"Say dat, Unc!" said Kevin.

Things started to pick up for the next few months, and we were getting back to where we started. Infrastructure around the world was built back up with the help of construction workers, volunteers, big businesses, and, surprisingly, Elisian technology. We saw through the news that the Elisians were teaching people on the fly how to use the technology, and it was working. This kind of catastrophe would've normally taken many, many years to fix, but we didn't have to worry about that.

Because of the vast improvements in our society within a short time, we were able to go back home. We left our stay in Long Island with our uncle and headed back to Westchester, but I knew going back to a rebuilt home wouldn't be the same. Yeah, it was nice that our house would have brand new renovations, but all of the things that reminded us of our childhood home were gone: the family photos, baby pictures, the nostalgic furniture. We got to the house and entered a brand new gift of a renovated home.

"Wow! Look at this, guys. I love it already, and we haven't seen the entire house yet!" screamed my father.

"It's beautiful!" said my mother.

"Ayo, what up *MTV Cribs*, this Killa Kev in the flesh, and welcome to my crib!" said Kevin to himself and the imaginary camera.

"Now, boys, I know that the old house and its memorabilia is no longer here, and a lot of memories created were lost, but think of this new place as a fresh start for a new life. Besides, the past is always in our minds, and you can always revert back to your brain for those memories," said my mother.

"Yeah, you're right, Mom," said Kev.

He turned towards me, grabbed me by the shirt and said, "AJ, c'mon man; cheer up, dawg! We got basically a brand new crib. Just like Moms said, bro: We can always remember the past, but the present and the future is what we gotta focus on."

"You're right, you're right, Kev," I said.

"Besides, all that shit you dealt with in the past won't be forgotten, but it also doesn't define you, dawg. We're heroes now with a new home, a new way of life, and hundreds of millions of supporters around the world. Isn't that everything you could ask for?" asked Kevin.

"Nah, what I wanted was to do it all with my family," I said.

Kevin smiled and pressed the top of my head with his hand in a circular motion like I was his little brother or something.

I went on to enjoy our new house, but I also enjoyed the new life I had as well. It was hectic with the immense attention and love we were receiving from the public every time we left the house! I forgot that we were high-profile public figures at this point, so maybe hiring security would've been a good idea.

Besides that, you could see the togetherness that people had with one another. Smiles filled the streets everywhere you looked. All kinds of communities were rebuilt with new renovations, and people from different walks of life and races were bonding and creating an understanding of one another with no sense of judgment in sight.

The love was the same on Elise, too. My family and I traveled through the portal every night to see the Maxwells, Lucious, and the people of Elise, and we were welcomed with open arms every time. It was nice to finally see that the utopia that was Elise was translating onto Earth.

The amazing changes occurring within our new world truly brought joy to my life. I sat back for a moment, wondering if my job was done. Yeah, I still was going to be a prominent figure—not just on Elise, but on Earth as well—for a long time, but was there any true threat to the universe anymore? My questions would eventually have answers, but I had to just live in the moment and bask in universal peace for the time being.

Days passed in a blur as the entire family did press runs, and even Cameron got some camera time. We also had Phoenix's graduation to attend at the end of the week. But, before leaving for Phoenix's graduation, I received a letter in the mail. Surprisingly, it was from Insecurity. She stated in the letter that she wanted me, and only me, to visit her at Rikers Island as she had some important information. I was very reluctant to visit Insecurity, so I called Madam Serenity and Sir Concord to get their opinion on what I should do. The two of them suggested I have security escort me to the prison and see what it was that Insecurity had to offer, so that was my plan for the next day.

CHAPTER 11
REAL BAD NEWS

Rikers Island is a prominent prison in America that houses many of the most dangerous criminals in the country, and I was going to step foot in there to visit the most dangerous person to ever exist.

I took a ride down to Rikers with private security accompanying me. When I reached the prison, my security couldn't enter because they weren't listed as visitors, so they had to wait until I was done meeting with Insecurity. I passed through security and waited in the visitation room. Insecurity was escorted in by the guards with a big, creepy smile on her face.

The shackles were taken off of her, and she sat down across from me.

"AJ, you actually came," said Insecurity.

"Well, of course I did. You said you had something important to share with me, so let's get right to it," I said.

She leaned over and whispered in my ear, and what she told me was shocking.

"You can't be serious, Insecurity," I said.

"Very serious, AJ," she responded.

She handed me a letter that she had received from an anonymous source. I began to read it, and what I read was not good.

"This is what I both wanted but didn't want to hear, Insecurity," I said. "Phoenix's graduation is in three days.

You know I can't tell the Maxwells and the world this news before her big day!"

"Then tell them after," said Insecurity.

"I need to know that you're not bullshitting me right now. Is everything you told me true?" I asked.

"Dude, I swear on my life and yours," she said. "What I do need, though, is a deal. Prison isn't all that bad for me, you know, but I'd like to see the blue sky and smell the fresh air and be in my normal clothes instead of an orange jumpsuit and cuffs."

"So, what are you asking, specifically?" I asked.

"I need supervised release. Tell the president to relocate me to the middle of nowhere—somewhere outdoorsy like Washington—but with security, of course. Can you do that for me?" asked Insecurity.

"I'll talk to him and see what he'll do for you, but no guarantees, so don't get your hopes up," I said.

A guard walked over and said that our time was up, so our conversation ended there. We both got up, and Insecurity was put back in cuffs and led out of the visitation room.

I left Rikers with my security, and for the next two days, my mind jumbled like marbles. When peace finally settled in, something always found its way back to ruin it. Before I questioned if I really had anything left to do for the universe as the chosen one, another problem arrived. I wasn't really good at holding onto things when I was super stressed, but I had to make sure I waited until after Phoenix's graduation to tell the president and the Maxwells what we had in store.

Days passed, and it was finally Phoenix's graduation day. The Maxwells had scheduled a charter for us that morning to fly into the San Francisco International Airport. When we landed, we were met by security and multiple all-black Cadillac SUVs that were there to escort us to the graduation.

"Oh, high school graduation! Good times. A very exciting moment," said my mom.

"Next year, that will be you two," said my father, pointing at Kev and me.

"Yeah, and you know what, Pops? I gotta start thinking about what I want to do after high school, like college or something," said Kevin.

"That's a great idea, son; what about you, AJ?" asked my father.

I was nervous to answer. Because of what I knew, and they didn't, college was probably gonna be on the back burner for a lot of people, but I had to say something to move on from the conversation.

"College! Yeah. You know, furthering my education, meeting new people, joining a fraternity where hopefully they aren't douchebags. All that fun stuff!" I said.

"Well, I'm glad you two are thinking about this stuff now. It's important," said my mom.

The conversation ended there, and we continued on our way to the graduation. We reached the high school's back entrance, where we met up with Sir Concord and Madam Serenity so we could dodge the cameras and unwanted attention.

"It's nice to see that you all could make it," said Serenity.

"You know we wouldn't miss Phoenix's big day," said my mom.

"Madam Serenity, may I pull you to the side before we go in? I have something important to tell you," I said.

"Sure! You guys go inside, and the two of us will catch up with you," said Serenity.

I felt like I couldn't wait any longer to tell someone the news I received from Insecurity, and I had to tell the lady in charge of Elise.

"Madam Serenity, I know it's your daughter's graduation, and I'm very excited for her just like you are, but I need to tell you something," I said.

"Of course, AJ! What is it that you have to tell me?" asked Serenity.

I had a scared look on my face, and she could then sense that it was something bad. I thought, *What if I tell her without telling her?* What if I just mentioned the good news and then hinted at the bad news without saying exactly what it was.

"So, I went and visited Insecurity at Rikers a couple days ago, and she told me some good news and bad news that you need to hear," I said.

"Okay, go ahead; spill the beans!" said Serenity.

"So, the good news is that Insecurity has a serum she's hidden for a long time which brings revival amongst the dead. She calls it the excito serum. She told me she has enough for thirty million people, which is ten million more than the casualty numbers. She made it for her people in battle but didn't need to use it."

"Has it been tested on humans?" asked Serenity.

"No, but I think we should just take a chance at this point," I said.

"Okay, so what's the bad news, AJ?"

"She's received calls and an anonymous letter from someone claiming they were from Planet Animus saying that they've infiltrated Iniquitous and are targeting not just Elise but Earth as well."

"And you believe her?" asked Serenity.

"Yeah, she showed me the note and looked scared, too, so this is a serious issue," I said.

Serenity looked concerned. "It can't be possible. I have never heard of Animus before. There are only a few planets in the galaxy, and Animus is definitely not one of them."

"Well, the only way to find out is if we go to Iniquitous ourselves," I said.

Serenity nodded her head, and we agreed to go into the ceremony with smiles on our faces and deal with the issue after. We walked in and joined my family and Concord in the front row as Phoenix's principal gave an intro speech and the students began to walk the stage. I was truly tuned out to the whole ceremony until the gift from God walked across the stage. She was stunning in her cap and gown with her luscious dark hair flowing, and my eyes got lost as always staring at her. I then looked over at Serenity and Concord; they began to stand up, and so did my family.

"Whoooo! Go Phoenix, go Phoenix, go Phoenix!" they all said collectively.

Everyone else in the ceremony stood up as well and chimed in. I—the only one sitting and looking lost—got up as well and joined the chant. Overall, the ceremony was a great event and experience. People's children were moving into the next step of their lives, and it was a great atmosphere to be a part of. Phoenix came down from the stage and joined the rest of us on the floor.

"Congratulations, honey. You're finally a high school graduate!" said Serenity.

"Congratulations, baby girl; you make us proud," said Concord.

"Thanks, Mom and Dad. You two helped me stay focused along the way," Phoenix responded.

"Way to go, Phoenix," said my mom and dad.

Kevin looked at Phoenix and gave her a head nod while Lil Man gave her a hug.

All of a sudden, Concord told Phoenix to share some news. "Hey Phoenix, don't you have some good news to tell AJ and the Hendrixes?"

Serenity looked at me in worry, like she knew I might be disappointed in what she had to say.

Phoenix smiled, and her eyes got big as she spilled the tea. "So, I had a ton of acceptance letters from different schools, and I thought about staying in California, but I decided to go to school in…."

"New York," I said in a low-toned voice.

She screamed, "Yes! I got into NYU, and I'm going in the fall. That means we can see each other, AJ! Isn't that great?"

Everybody else looked excited as they were very happy for her, which I was too, but only Serenity and I knew that it wasn't going to happen.

"Yeah, that's amazing, Phoenix. That's great," I responded.

"What's wrong, AJ? You don't have that pep in your step like you usually do. You know, you should follow that vegan diet I texted you last week. It'll help you feel more lively."

"Oh no, Phoenix. I'm fine, just a little jet-lagged, and besides, black bean burgers are definitely not my thing," I said.

"Well, don't blame me when I keep kicking your ass in training," Phoenix responded.

"Enough of the chit-chat. Let's go back to the house. We have dinner and cake waiting for us all," said Concord.

The rest of the day was internally dreadful because I knew we had defeated one source of evil to restore peace back on Earth just for another one to potentially wreak havoc on our world. It was very difficult for Serenity and me to keep a smile on our faces during Phoenix's celebration. We knew we had to let everyone and the president know about the potential threat infiltrating our lives. We ate dinner, had cake for dessert, and danced to music to end the night.

We all were getting ready for bed as my family was set to head back to New York, but that wasn't going to happen. As everyone went upstairs, Madam Serenity stayed in the kitchen. I went over to her to have a chat.

"So, what are we going to do, Serenity?" I asked.

"AJ, we have to tell them. I know we ended my daughter's special day on a high, but we have to get back to reality. People's lives might be at stake again, and we don't have time to wait. We have to get on this right now! Get on the phone with the president and tell him what's going on. After you're done, let me know," said Serenity.

"You got it," I responded.

I trotted down to the basement just to make sure there wasn't a chance of anyone overhearing my conversation with the president. I dialed the number, stated my credentials, and got transferred right to him.

"Hello?" said the president.

"Hey, Mr. President, it's AJ, and I have something very important to disclose to you," I said.

"Oh, AJ! One of my favorite people around! It's nice to hear from you. So, what is the important thing that you have to share with me?"

"Well, Mr. President, what I have to share is quite alarming."

"Oh geez. Well, go on, AJ. what is it?" asked the president.

"I recently visited Insecurity at Rikers, and she gave me information and a written letter from a potential imminent threat on their way to Elise and Earth. Apparently, someone from Planet Animus has infiltrated Iniquitous and is targeting us next," I told him.

"AJ, I'm going to alert our global defense because I trust you, but after your public address, I need you to go to Iniquitous and confirm that everything is accurate," said the president.

"Will do, Mr. President, and one more thing before we end our call. Insecurity asked me for a favor in return for her cooperation. She has held onto a revival serum called the excito serum that can bring back all of the casualties from the massacre. She has a supply of thirty million doses, which is more than enough for all of the individuals lost. In return, she wants you to grant her supervised release to a secluded location for the remainder of her sentence."

"AJ, is she crazy?! There's no way I'm allowing her supervised release after what she did. She's lucky to even be alive ."

"Mr. President, please consider this. Without her serum and the letter, we would all be doomed pretty soon," I said.

"Fuck! You know what, AJ? Fine, I'll grant her supervised release, but with top-notch national security. We still have to treat her as a threat."

"Understood, Mr. President. She also requested to be relocated to a woodsy area like Washington State," I responded.

"That's fine. We have a location for her out there; don't worry about it. We'll do a virtual public address and broadcast it nationally, but after the address, you go to Iniquitous. Bring Insecurity with you, and let me know if we're in trouble," said the president.

I reassured him, and we ended our call there. I ran from the basement and back up the steps to tell Serenity.

"So, what did he say?" she asked.

"Instead of heading home, I'll do the public address from here. After that, Insecurity will come with us to Iniquitous to see if what the letter said was true, so I think it's best we gather everyone downstairs to tell them the news. I also think you should rally the Elisians because we might be in for it."

Serenity screamed at the top of her lungs for everyone to come downstairs. My family, along with Phoenix and Concord, filed down the steps as we stood in front of them to spread the bad news.

"Ayo, what's going on? What's the issue?" asked Kevin.

"Is everything alright, Mom?" asked Phoenix.

"As much as it hurts to say this, everything isn't okay, and AJ will tell you why."

"When I went to visit Insecurity at Rikers, she told me that she has received threats from someone claiming they're from another planet and have destroyed her home. Not only that; they are seeking to take over Elise and Earth next, and if they've destroyed Iniquitous, we're in trouble," I said.

"What the fuck, fam! Forreal, dawg, what the fuck is going on? We finally get back to normal just for someone to come fuck it up again! Geez, AJ," said Kevin.

Everybody's faces were in complete disbelief and disappointment. A good day had just turned bad in less than 24 hours, and it was going to be worse once the world found out the next day.

"I thought I was going to college, going to live it up in New York and spend time with my man. Why, AJ? Why does this have to happen now?" said Phoenix in distress.

"Babes, I know it's not the ideal situation once again, but we've got to do what we've got to do. Once we tackle this issue, we'll be back to normal in no time," I said.

It was hard to stay positive with the unknown lingering over our heads. Before we dispersed for the night, Concord said he would travel through the portal to warn the people of Elise once again.

I couldn't sleep for the rest of the night. My eyes stared at the ceiling, and I couldn't close them. It was like my eyelids were stapled to the back of my head. I was so battered that I didn't even want to sleep in the guest rooms, and I rested on the couch in the living area. I just wanted peace. I was sick and tired of being sick and tired. I needed to make a bigger mark and impact than I did defending the world before, and my first step was to make a statement in the public address that would hit the world hard.

The morning sun rose, and still with no sleep, I managed to get off of the couch and help myself to some coffee. I never really had coffee, but I'd seen Serenity make it in the coffee machine, and it seemed easy. I grabbed the mocha flavor since I loved chocolate and helped myself to a cup.

Madam Serenity came down alongside my mother and approached me. "I see you helped yourself to some coffee. I never knew you drink coffee," she said.

"I don't, but I need it right now. I didn't get any sleep at all last night," I said.

"Well, the news camera crew is coming here in a bit to help set up for your public address, just to let you know," she said.

"Junior, Serenity told us everything this morning while you were sleeping on the couch. I know it's a stressful time and a lot of pressure on you once again, but you just have to take everything day by day, son," said my mother.

I hugged her and thanked her for her words of encouragement. Growing up, I was told that mothers are always right, and I knew she was. I just had to take it day by day, try my best and accept the outcome.

A few hours passed with all of us gathering for breakfast, Phoenix pestering me about her college dreams while joking about how dead I looked, Kevin talking to Shelby on the phone nonstop, Lil Man running around the house, the camera crew getting everything situated and the adults just chilling, waiting for me to go live.

More time passed, and it was finally time to give my public address. The president called me prior to prep before we broadcasted. He was set to speak first and then myself.

"Good morning, my fellow Americans and all the viewers across the world. We have endured a tough year together. Many people lost loved ones, morale was in a dumpster, and many of us lost hope for life in general, but we came together with the help of the Elisians to restore our world back to where it needed to be. I have AJ Hendrix here to inform you all on another very important matter."

The camera then cut to me, and I began to speak. "My fellow people, there is some news that I have to share with you. I got word from Insecurity a few days ago that we might potentially be dealing with another imminent threat to our world. I know we have just gotten through tough times, but I think this will make us tougher. Before I knew I would be chosen to help save the world, I was a nobody. Stepping out of my household, out of the comfort of my home and my family, I felt non-existent. I was discriminated against, picked on and felt ostracized from my peers.

"I felt like quitting, but I realized there was one thing that I cherished so much, one thing that kept me going and still keeps me motivated to live through life each and every day, and that was my family. What I'm trying to say is for the ones who've felt lost in life, for the people who have no hope for their future, what I need you to do is find something that motivates you to not only improve yourself but that inspires you to not quit and to live life to the fullest. For this potential battle we may have to come across once again, I need all of you to find that one motivating factor and prepare to fight for your purpose and your life because each and every one of you matters. That's all I have to say, and I'm out."

My mic-drop-like statement caused the broadcast to shift from me back to the president, and then the news crew shut the cameras off. They then packed up their stuff and left out the door as Phoenix and Kevin ran down the steps to show me the instant reaction from social media that people around the world were having to my speech.

"AJ, you're getting a lot of love right now, bro," said Kevin.

"Yeah, Junior, it seems that a lot of people felt your words like they really resonated with them," said Phoenix.

"A lot of them are ready to go fight too, fam, on some *Call of Duty* shit. No one's scared this time," said Kevin.

It was great to see people weren't afraid and were willing to stand their ground and prepare for imminent danger.

All of a sudden, my mother ran to me like Usain Bolt in a 100-meter dash.

"Insecurity! They're flying her over here!"

"Oh, hell nah. Why'd they release her from jail? Ayo, Phoenix, you better sock that evil bitch in her mouth, straight up," said Kevin. He caught himself and immediately apologized. "My apologies for saying bitch, but she still don't got my forgiveness."

My mother then began to speak, "Son, no need to apologize, she's an evil..." then Phoenix and my mother said simultaneously, "Bitch!"

With me crashing from my cup of coffee, I managed to get a few words in.

"Calm down, guys. She's coming with us to retrieve the serum. If she doesn't come with us, we won't know our way around Iniquitous, and we won't get it."

"Okay, fine, babes. But I'm not saying a word to her, and I don't want to hear any of that 'auntie' bullshit 'cause I don't know her," said Phoenix.

"Yeah, no lie, AJ; you crazy, bro, for trusting that chick. She forreal psycho, dawg," said Kevin.

"Everyone just chill for a couple hours, and we'll wait till she gets here, alright?" I said.

They all agreed, and we sat down on the couches until we heard loud footsteps coming from the basement. Concord ran up the steps, and next to him, to my surprise, was Lucious! My dad, mom, Kev, and everyone else screamed, "Lucious!"

"Lucious, how did you get here?" asked my dad.

"Sir Concord miraculously had a spare pair of glasses and he gave them to me. He always knew I wanted to come back to Earth, and he said since I've been working so hard, it was time."

"Yeah, that's right. I've had a spare pair for the longest time. I held onto them just in case I needed them, but Lucious deserved them," said Concord.

I walked up to Lucious with all the energy I had left and said, "Lucious, it's nice to finally see you on Ear...."

Suddenly, the ground felt lopsided, everything was blurry, and my legs and arms felt like spaghetti. A few seconds later, I hit the ground so hard like Mick Foley in the Hell in a Cell match.

CHAPTER 12
JUST THE BEGINNING

Right away, I was back on my paradise island: the glass house with the red sandy beach, the big bedroom, my white robe. But this time, there were no beautiful women walking around my crib because the only beautiful woman I needed in life was laying right next to me in her white robe with two cups of coffee in her hand.

"Good morning, babe. How'd you sleep?" asked Phoenix.

"Pretty well, to be honest. Is that cup for me?" I asked.

"Yeah, it is, but you better get your ass off this bed because I made breakfast," said Phoenix.

"Say no more, babes," I responded.

I got off of the bed and headed down the spiral steps with Phoenix. Walking into the kitchen, my eyes lit up like a Christmas tree.

It was like an all-out buffet! Pancakes, bacon, sausage, waffles, any breakfast food you could think of. I was in breakfast heaven with all of this food. I asked Phoenix how she made all of it.

"Phoenix, when did you learn how to cook?"

"Overnight," she laughed.

"Well, babes, I just want to say thank you for doing this for me," I said.

"No problem, AJ, but you know what I need you to do for me?" she asked.

"Yeah, sure, what is it?" I said.

"Wake up, wake up, wake up," Phoenix kept saying.

"What are you talking about?" I asked.

She continued to say it over and over again, and it got really creepy. I got up out of my seat and stared at her. Suddenly, my brothers, Lucious, my parents, her parents, and, surprisingly, Insecurity and two huge secret service security guards popped up and joined in with Phoenix.

I began to get annoyed by the chants, so I screamed, "Shut up!"

Then, everything went black. I could faintly hear the chants again.

"Wake up, wake up, wake up, wake up."

The darkness changed to light as I woke up, staring at everyone looking down at me on the couch.

"Hey, AJ," said Insecurity.

"Woah, when did you get here? I thought you weren't supposed to get here for five hours?" I asked.

"Well, actually three hours, and you've been knocked out for a little longer than that," Insecurity said while in cuffs.

Kevin said, "Yeah, and you were talking in your sleep the whole time, on some 'Phoenix, you don't know how much I truly appreciate you, you inspire me every day, I love you' shit. Like damn, I know shawty makes you happy, but this ain't no soap opera, broski."

"It was a little cringey, but it was very cute, and you know I love you, too. The love is always reciprocated," said Phoenix.

"Sir, if I may, I think we should head on our way to Iniquitous now," said Lucious.

"Agreed. Come on, everyone. Let's head out," said Concord. He then looked at the security guards and reassured them that Insecurity was no threat to them and that they could stay back.

My little brother stayed back with the sitter along with my parents as the rest of us took off into the huge Hillsborough backyard and got in two separate drones. Insecurity got in one with Kev, Phoenix and I, and Sir Concord and Madam Serenity got in their own drone. Phoenix took charge of flying as we took off into the sky.

"I wonder if Iniquitous looks the same as how we left it," said Kevin.

"Shut up!" said Insecurity.

"You shut up, crazy girl. You tried to end the world and failed," said Kevin.

"Kev, shut the fuck up, okay? I don't want any bickering from anybody. We're going to get the serum and see if any more damage was done to Iniquitous," I said.

"Okay, okay. You're right, AJ. My bad," said Kevin.

We continued to soar through the sky at high speed, leaving Earth and passing by planet after planet, even Elise. Time passed, and we finally reached Iniquitous. Unfortunately, what we saw was even worse than before. There were even more dead bodies on the ground. Once we landed the drones, Insecurity ran out, bawling.

"Oh no, this can't be happening, this can't be happening. Why, why, why?" screamed Insecurity.

"Karma's a bitch, ain't it," said Kevin.

I punched Kevin in the arm and asked, "You know this isn't good for us, don't you?" I said.

"Yeah, I know. My fault, G, my fault," said Kevin.

Concord and Serenity exited their drone with disappointed looks on their faces.

"Well, Insecurity, someone was definitely here, so we need you to lead us to your castle to see if they still are," said Concord.

"Sure, sure. Follow me this way," said Insecurity.

We all walked miles and miles to get to her castle, and Kevin and Phoenix weren't feeling it.

"Why couldn't we just fly over there?" asked Phoenix.

"Yeah, this walking shit is not the wave," said Kevin.

"Well, I figured if we flew, we would attract attention if there was someone here," said Insecurity.

"You know, she's right, even though I hate to admit it," said Madam Serenity.

We continued to walk until the castle was in sight, and surrounding the castle were even bigger drones than what we had. This was just a guarantee that Iniquitous was infiltrated and a new war was among us. But who were the people from Planet Animus? We had to look at what we were going up against without being spotted, and we knew that was going to be a challenge.

Insecurity obviously knew her way around, so we circled the castle and hid in some dark spots where we wouldn't be seen. We saw three big dudes at the front entrance with guns in their hands, just chopping it up and laughing. It angered Insecurity so much that she lunged out of our hiding spot and attacked the three of them by herself. She was laying the smackdown on them, and even though we all got out of hiding to help, she didn't need it. She knocked all three out with karate kicks since her hands were still cuffed, and I was able to collect their guns, which I handed off to Phoenix, Lucious, and Kevin.

"Ooh, crazy lady knows how to fight!" said Kevin.

"Enough of that. Let's go inside! I need to get my home back," screamed Insecurity.

We went inside, and who we saw sitting on Insecurity's throne was mind blowing!

"Ain't no way. Ain't no way," I said.

"This has to be a joke. This can't be real, sir," said Lucious.

"Look in his hand. I think the serum is in the case," said Phoenix.

I looked at Insecurity, and she was shocked. She jumped out of hiding and screamed, "Daddy?!"

"Mom, Dad, this is bad, isn't it?" asked Phoenix.

Everyone was in complete shock, and we couldn't really handle ourselves.

"AJ, you know we're fucked, right?" Kevin said to me.

At that moment, I couldn't believe the situation we were in. I had been so stressed by dealing with Insecurity, and now I didn't know how this would go. My prior adventures weren't the end-all-be-all to restoring peace to the world, and my journey of being the savior of the universe wasn't over. It was just getting started.